SHIELDING TALULLAH (SPECIAL FORCES: OPERATION ALPHA)

DELTA FORCE - GENERATION NEXT, BOOK 4

JEN TALTY

"Deadly Secrets is the best of romance and suspense in one hot read!" *NYT Bestselling Author Jennifer Probst*

"A charming setting and a steamy couple heat up the pages in a suspenseful story I couldn't put down!" *NY Times and USA today Bestselling Author Donna Grant*

"Jen Talty's books will grab your attention and pull you into a world of relatable characters, strong personalities, humor, and believable storylines. You'll laugh, you'll cry, and you'll rush to get the next book she releases!" Natalie Ann USA Today Bestselling Author

"I positively loved *In Two Weeks*, and highly

recommend it. The writing is wonderful, the story is fantastic, and the characters will keep you coming back for more. I can't wait to get my hands on future installments of the NYS Troopers series." *Long and Short Reviews*

"*In Two Weeks* hooks the reader from page one. This is a fast paced story where the development of the romance grabs you emotionally and the suspense keeps you sitting on the edge of your chair. Great characters, great writing, and a believable plot that can be a warning to all of us." *Desiree Holt, USA Today Bestseller*

"*Dark Water* delivers an engaging portrait of wounded hearts as the memorable characters take you on a healing journey of love. A mysterious death brings danger and intrigue into the drama, while sultry passions brew into a believable plot that melts the reader's heart. Jen Talty pens an entertaining romance that grips the heart as the colorful and dangerous story unfolds into a chilling ending." *Night Owl Reviews*

"This is not the typical love story, nor is it the typical mystery. The characters are well rounded and interesting." *You Gotta Read Reviews*

"*Murder in Paradise Bay* is a fast-paced romantic

thriller with plenty of twists and turns to keep you guessing until the end. You won't want to miss this one..." *USA Today bestselling author Janice Maynard*

Dear Readers,

Welcome to the Special Forces: Operation Alpha Fan-Fiction world!

If you are new to this amazing world, in a nutshell the author wrote a story using one or more of my characters in it. Sometimes that character has a major role in the story, and other times they are only mentioned briefly. This is perfectly legal and allowable because they are going through Aces Press to publish the story.

This book is entirely the work of the author who wrote it. While I might have assisted with brainstorming and other ideas about which of my characters to use, I didn't have any part in the process or writing or editing the story.

I'm proud and excited that so many authors loved my characters enough that they wanted to write them into their own story. Thank you for supporting them, and me!

READ ON!
 Xoxo
 Susan Stoker

CHAPTER 1

Doctor Talullah Rossi snagged the chart—no, two charts—from the wall and smiled.

All her patients were her favorite.

But not all the parents. It wasn't that she didn't appreciate all the moms and dads, but some were more needy than others. And some didn't like to follow her advice.

And then there were those who just thought they knew more than her medical degree. Those were always the most challenging. They came in armed with all the latest articles, ready to defend and challenge her no matter what she said.

However, Trigger Nelson and his wife, Gillian Romano, were two of the best people on the planet.

Not to mention that Trigger and the rest of his Delta Force team who had children came to her practice.

Not only that, but the men on his mirror team had started to bring their children to her and before she knew it; she'd start having to turn people away. She didn't actually like the idea of having to say no to new patients; however, it would be nice to be so popular that she had parents lining up out the door to be seen by her and her staff.

Not to mention she had a mortgage to deal with now. She probably should have given herself a little more breathing room between having paid off her school loans and using all her savings to buy a house, but she wanted a place to call her own. Something more than an apartment or rental. She wanted a space that felt like home.

It was hard for others to understand that a single woman could make a big house a home while living by herself. She didn't need a man to do that, but someday—preferably in the near future—she wanted someone to share her life with. Her sister warned her that sometimes her fierce independence could be intimidating; however, this was who she was and anyone who chose to be with her had to accept all the things that made up her personality.

She pulled her thoughts back to the present. The

twins were now five years old and getting ready for kindergarten. Amazing. Hard to believe it had been that long. She remembered how they had told her their story about trying to get pregnant in the first place.

Truly one of those happy moments in life.

She tapped on the door. "How is my favorite family?" One of the things that she loved about the Nelsons was that they always tried to make doctor visits a family affair.

Mom and Dad parented together.

Which meant sick visits and well visits; if Dad wasn't deployed, he was present.

Always.

"We're having a moment," Trigger said as he leaned against the counter.

"Someone doesn't like the word no." Gillian held Josie, who was wearing only her underpants, on her lap with a book, while Joe, in the same type of undergarment, sat on the exam table with his arms folded and sour puss on his face.

"Or share," Trigger said.

"I had it first," Joe said.

"Sharing wasn't an easy thing for me to do either when I was your age." Talullah kept her attention focused on Joe. "But it's the right thing to do."

3

"She took it right out of my hand."

"You were teasing your sister with it," Trigger said. "You know how I feel about that."

"Yes, sir," Joe said.

"Wow. You've grown a lot this year." Talullah redirected the conversation. "Are you ready to start school?"

"Daddy said I'm getting shots today. Is that true?" Joe asked in a highly intelligent voice.

"I'm afraid so." Talullah nodded.

"I told you." He stuck out his tongue as he turned his head and faced his sister who burst into tears.

"Joe. That's not nice," his father said, shaking his head. "I can't believe I did this, but we asked that they not be in the same class. Sometimes it's hard to believe that they're twins."

"This is all normal behavior for this age."

"I thought twins were supposed to be super close," Trigger said.

"They can be," she said. "Usually with twins, it's more like they have a sixth sense about one another. And other twins, like these two, are more typical brother-sister siblings."

"You mean like oil and water."

She laughed. "Something like that." She warmed her stethoscope. "Hey, Joe." She pressed it against his bare chest. "Your father's right. It's not nice to stick your tongue out and tease Josie like that. I'm sure you wouldn't want another boy to tease her like that, now would you?"

"No. But she didn't believe me," Joe protested.

"Me saying you were getting them was all the proof you needed." She moved her scope to the boy's back. So far everything sounded normal. Not that she expected anything to be different. She'd seen both kids recently for a summer stomach bug. Other than that, they were healthy.

She continued her examination of Joe, looking into his ears, checking his eyes and reflexes.

Nothing out of the ordinary.

She moved to Josie. She did that exam while Josie sat on her mother's lap.

Again, everything was just fine with both children.

"How's their diet?" she asked.

"He'll eat anything you put in front of him," Trigger stated. "He's a bottomless pit, but his sister is a little bit on the picky side and has some issues with food touching."

"That's not uncommon," Talullah said. "My advice is not to make a big deal about it and if she tosses a fit about it, don't give her a new plate. She's not going to go hungry."

"We're doing that, but it's hard sometimes," Gillian said. "She can be dramatic. As you can see."

"You're good parents. She might not outgrow drama. That seems to be a challenge for all kids, but as soon as you have this phase figured out, she'll be on to a new one."

"As long she never becomes boy crazy and stays daddy's little girl, we're good," Trigger said.

Talullah laughed. "I can see there might be some double standards in this house."

"You have no idea." Gillian rolled her eyes.

"Oh. Babe. That's not fair. My daughter will be able to take care of herself just like my boy. She's just not going to be allowed to date until I've done a full background check, that's all."

"I look forward to watching this play out." Talullah prepared the swabs and needles. She lowered herself to Josie's level and patted her on the back.

The little girl turned her head, resting it on her mother's shoulder.

"Now. I'm not going to lie. This will pinch a little bit. But it won't hurt more than a couple of seconds."

"No, Mommy!" Josie hugged Gillian, wrapping her little arms and legs around her mother tight.

"It's going to be okay," Gillian whispered as she ran her hands up and down her daughter's back.

Talullah stood and leaned against the exam table. She had to admit, this was one of the worst parts of her job. She knew that she wasn't hurting children. She was protecting them, but the shots did sting. She glanced to Trigger for guidance. "Which one first?" she asked softly. "You know your kids better than I do. My instinct is to go with Joe, but something tells me he's full of bravado."

Trigger inched closer to his son, resting his hand on the boy's thigh. "You're right about that. But he'll be brave. Won't you, son?"

"Yes, sir." Joe nodded like a bobblehead.

"Okay. So, we've got two shots today." She rubbed Joe's thigh. "And I hate to mention this, but then we have two more we need to do in a couple of months."

"I've got it on my calendar," Gillian said. "Appointment has already been made."

"Okay, Joe. A little pinch right here in your leg. And then again in the other one," Talullah said. "Take a big breath." Joe inhaled and closed his little eyes.

She quickly pinched his chunky thigh and injected the vaccine.

Joe opened his mouth but didn't cry. However, his face turned bright red.

"You're being so brave." Trigger took his son's hand and smiled.

Talullah repeated her motions on the second thigh, but this time Joe let out a little moan.

Josie didn't once glance up. She kept her head buried in her mother's neck.

"That wasn't too bad now, was it, Joe?" Talullah said.

"No, ma'am," Joe said and then sniffled.

"Okay, Josie. It's your turn."

The little girl whined.

"Just do it," Gillian said.

Talullah went about her business and she was surprised by how Josie didn't flinch. She groaned a little, but that was about it.

"Okay. The twins can get dressed," Talullah said. "Do you have any questions for me?"

"We do," Trigger said. "Can we put them in the TV room?"

"Of course. That's what it's there for." One of the things that Talullah thought made her practice unique had been the ability for her to talk to parents while the children were well taken care of in a separate room.

Talullah hired staff to stay in the TV room so that parents felt comfortable using it. It meant her paycheck was a little less, but it was well worth it and almost all the parents used it on a regular basis.

Her partners had been skeptical at first, but they were fully on board and pooled their resources now as well.

She cleaned up the area while Trigger and Gillian sent their kids off with a sugar-free sucker. "From a medical standpoint, your children are doing great. Both growing at the proper rate and their hearing and eyesight appear to be good. Is there something specific about their development you wanted to discuss?"

"Actually," Gillian started. "This is more personal than professional."

Trigger raised his hands. "I want you to know that this is mostly my wife's idea."

Gillian stood, smoothed down her slacks, and folded her arms across her chest. "You're the one who suggested Scout."

"I made a comment, not a suggestion." Trigger held up hand as if he were defending himself. "You're the one who went full-court press on this."

Talullah was mildly amused by their banter. She'd become friendly with Gillian and they occasionally saw each other at Talullah's yoga studio. A few times they'd gotten a juice after class and chatted and had planned on getting together for a girls' night sometime. However, they often went at different times because of work schedules, so they had yet to schedule something.

"But you have to admit, he's perfect for her," Gillian said.

"Wait, what?" Talullah blinked. "Who's perfect for me?"

"Our friend, Scout," Gillian said with a big smile. She had this glow about her that made her look like the happiest person in the room. "I really think you'll like him."

"Are you trying to fix me up?" About two weeks ago, she'd confided in Gillian about how frustrated she'd been over the dating scene. She hadn't done that with the hopes of being introduced to someone; she only wanted to vent about how bad the last few men she'd gone out with had been.

"Don't look at it that way," Trigger said. "We're simply introducing you to a great guy. If you hit it off, that's awesome. If you don't." He shrugged. "Then there's no harm. You go your separate ways."

It wasn't always that easy. She shivered. She'd gone on one date with Kyle Diel. She knew he wasn't going to be anyone she wanted to spend her time with, but she agreed so he'd stop asking. That had been a couple of weeks ago.

Silly her thought he'd see they weren't compatible and he'd leave her alone. She thought if she showed him while they were having dinner that they had nothing in common and that she wasn't the right girl for him, he'd move on.

Nope. He'd texted her on a regular basis asking her on a second date. Or if he wasn't asking, he was acting as if they were best friends or already in a relationship. At first, she politely responded, but turned him down anytime he wanted to get together. Now she did her best to ignore him, without being rude.

That had become almost impossible.

She dreaded the day he made a sales call to the office. That usually happened the first week of every month, which meant he was due in a few days.

Wonderful.

This was why she shouldn't date anyone who did business with her practice compounded with the fact he and his ex-wife had a child under her care.

What a stupid mistake. She'd have to be firm with him the next time he asked.

Although, she had a feeling that with Kyle, it would be better if she did it in person.

"I appreciate that you thought of me, but I don't think it would be a good idea for me to go on a blind date with a patient's friend." The last thing she wanted to do was insult her favorite family, but after what happened with Kyle, she didn't want to give anyone the wrong impression. However, she had to admit she was intrigued. Had she followed her gut instincts and said no to Kyle, she would have said yes to this one.

"We can do this one of three ways," Trigger said. "You can go out with him by yourself. The four of us can go out. Or you can come to our house for a barbecue where lots of people will be."

"Some of whom will be Trigger's buddies and other families from the base. You know many of them, so you couldn't even call it a date." Gillian held up her cell. "Before you decide, take a look."

Talullah's pulse found its way to her throat. Heat rose from her toes to her cheeks. She felt her eyes widen. Her muscles tightened with a heightened sense of desire.

"I know, right. He's sexy."

"Um. Husband standing only a few feet away." Trigger lifted his hand and pointed his index finger over his head. He laughed. "Though, if I liked men, I might be interested."

Talullah couldn't help it, she burst out laughing. For as long as she'd known Trigger, he'd had an incredibly dry sense of humor. He always managed to land a one-liner right at the precise moment everyone could use a chuckle.

"No. I mean it. And it's not only because he's handsome. He's good people. The best." Trigger smiled. "What harm can going on one date do?"

"Do you mind if I ask a few questions?" She couldn't believe she was even entertaining this after everything she'd been going through with Kyle. She'd sworn off men for a few months. Not forever because she could feel her biological clock ticking, although she didn't need to be in a relationship to have a child. But she wanted to do things the old-fashioned way if she could.

"Go right ahead," Trigger said. "I would do the same thing if I were you."

"Has he ever been married?" Not that it would have mattered. She had a few friends who married young and it didn't work out. Shit happened. No judgment there.

"Nope," Gillian said. "He did have a girlfriend for a little over a year. Scout said they broke up because she didn't take to military life and he wasn't ready to leave it which meant he didn't love her like he should."

Talullah found it interesting that Scout would describe his feelings as not enough to sustain a relationship over the long haul. It showed self-awareness, which she admired.

"So, I take it he doesn't have kids." She certainly wouldn't be opposed to getting involved with someone who had a child, but that did complicate matters.

"He does not. But he's great with our twins," Trigger added. "He's got one sister. She's married. His parents are in the hospitality industry. They come to town once in a while and we've met them all. Nice people."

"I don't think he's got any major skeletons, if that's what you're fishing for," Gillian said. "Why not just come to our gathering instead of going on a date?"

Talullah took a moment to weigh all the options.

Scout had sex appeal. She couldn't deny that. Gillian and Trigger weren't the kind of people who would set her up with a crazy person. She had promised her sister that she'd get back out there, only that was before Kyle had made her want to crawl under a rock and hibernate for a few months.

This was one of those opportunities she shouldn't pass on.

The only question that remained was should she go on a date alone with Scout? Or go to the party because a double date was out of the question.

The party could end up being a bunch of parents asking her questions about their children, which could be a saving grace if the date ended up being horrible and she had nothing in common with Scout.

Or she could end up in a corner by herself while Scout hung out with her buddies.

"You only live once," she said. "I'll go out with him." She scribbled her cell on a piece of paper. "Tell him to give me a call to set something up."

"That's great. You won't regret it," Trigger said.

"One more question." She gripped the door handle. "What have you told him about me?"

Trigger tapped the center of his chest. "I told him that you're my kids' doctor and that you're the best in town, so he better be on his best behavior or I might have to beat the crap out of him."

"He actually said that." Gillian nodded. "But

mostly we talked up how nice you are and how wonderful you are with the kids. Scout's looking forward to meeting you."

Talullah pulled open the door. "I'll see you in a couple of months for the flu and chicken pox vaccines. After that, hopefully the twins will remain healthy until their next well visit."

"Or maybe we'll be seeing you on the arm of our friend." Trigger winked.

"I suppose anything is possible." She stood in the hallway and waited for them to collect the twins, who turned and waved.

She smiled, blowing them each a kiss. Seeing the children thrive and grow was the most rewarding part of her job.

"Excuse me," Teresa, one of the receptionists, said as she rounded the corner. "Kyle Diel is here to drop off some samples. He was hoping to speak with you. Oh, and before I forget, Wayne left for the day."

Talullah groaned. She glanced at her watch. The twins had been her last appointment for the day. She had about an hour's worth of paperwork before heading home for a glass of wine and maybe a soak in the spa before ordering dinner.

Or maybe she'd just have a salad.

"Did Kyle say what he wanted?" Talullah asked.

Too bad Wayne had left. If he were still in the office, he would have told Kyle to turn around and leave, or at the very least given him some excuse about how she was busy and couldn't see him. Teresa struggled with coming up with excuses.

But not Wayne.

"He didn't and when I pressed, he said he preferred to discuss it with you." Teresa pursed her lips. "I'm sorry."

"Don't worry about it. I'll take care of Kyle." No way was she going to take this one in her office. If he wasn't dropping off medical supplies, then too bad. This wasn't a scheduled visit and she'd been clear the last time he did this that she didn't have time in her schedule for unannounced appointments.

She squared her shoulders and stepped into the lobby. "Hi, Kyle," she said. "Thank you for taking the time to bring the supplies over today. It wasn't necessary. We had enough to get us through until your next scheduled visit."

"It was on my way home, so it's absolutely no problem." Kyle leaned against the counter and smiled.

She cringed. While he was an attractive man with his chocolate eyes, thick wavy hair, and what appeared to be a solid body, his personality left something to be desired. He wasn't funny, but he thought he was, and he had a sense of arrogance that she didn't feel was deserving. He also spent most of the time talking about himself and he rarely asked questions or seemed interested in other people, unless it served his purpose.

"Since it's Friday, and close to the end of the day, I was hoping that maybe we could go out for a cocktail or something."

"I'm sorry, but I'm not done with work and I have plans tonight." Liar, liar, pants on fire. Okay, it wasn't a total fib. The first part was absolutely true and the latter, well, she had made plans.

With herself.

"Perhaps we can chat in your office." He waved his hand. "I promise not to take too much of your time."

He's going to make her do this right there in the middle of her workplace with half her staff awkwardly trying not to notice what was happening.

"I'm really busy. Now isn't a good time."

He had the nerve to reach out and squeeze her biceps, guiding her away from the reception desk.

She gritted her teeth. "Kyle," she said softly.

He leaned closer. "Let's take this where it's a little more private."

She blew out a puff of air. "This is highly unprofessional," she said firmly.

He narrowed his stare. "I'm going to head over to Oscar's. Why don't you join me when you're done with whatever it is you need to finish up with here?"

There was no way that was going to happen.

She walked him to entrance and opened the door. "I'm sorry, but like I said, I have plans tonight." She pulled it closed, locking it and turning to Teresa. "Any other patients left in the office? Is anyone else seeing any other patients this afternoon?" She was one of three doctors in the practice. While she was done with her work for the day, that didn't mean there weren't others coming.

"Everyone is done for the day," Teresa said. "He does not understand the word no."

Talullah exhaled. "I should have never given in and gone out with him in the first place."

"I'm going to add insult to injury." Teresa came out from around the reception desk. "I heard from a mutual friend that he's filed for full custody and Elaine is freaking out. Rightfully so, if you ask me."

"I didn't know things had gotten that heated." Talullah did know that the divorce was ugly. That his ex-wife had cheated on him—or at least that is what he had told her—but he hadn't wanted to get divorced. He had wanted to try marriage counseling and all that good stuff.

But Elaine had refused.

The way he talked, Elaine had single-handedly destroyed their relationship and was now doing her best to poison their eight-year-old daughter against him.

Talullah had never once discussed this with Elaine who in turn had never brought it up with Talullah, except to ask about a referral to a child psychologist for her daughter. Otherwise, Elaine remained tight-lipped when she brought their daughter into the office.

However, Talullah didn't believe half of what came out of Kyle's mouth anymore. She used to feel bad for him, but the more she listened to him, the more she realized he was full of shit.

"My friend said that if she's even fifteen minutes late for drop-off or pickup, he's calling the cops. And he flipped out on her when he found out her fiancé was spending time with Brittany." Teresa took a stack of files from the desk. "Anyway. While Elaine admits to her part in the breakup of their marriage, I don't think he's got his head on straight."

Talullah had to agree. But none of it was her business and if Kyle didn't take the hint when she didn't show up tonight, she'd have to do what her father called *flipping the bitch switch.*

"Thanks for the tip," she said. "I have some paperwork to do in my office if you need me." Thank goodness she'd remembered to put a bottle of her favorite white wine in the fridge before she'd left for work this morning. Unpacking had been a bitch and it had been going slower than usual. Her family thought she'd been nuts in buying a house with no husband, and no prospects of a husband.

However, why did she need a man to enjoy the comforts of a home?

She stepped into her office and pulled her cell from her desk drawer.

One missed call with a voice message. She didn't recognize the number. She tapped the playback button.

"Hi, Talullah. This is Scout, Trigger's friend."

Her heart smacked into the back of her throat. She gripped the side of her desk for support so she didn't crumple to the floor.

She figured the man would call.

In a couple of days.

Maybe a week.

Not in half an hour.

She' wasn't sure if that meant he was desperate.

Or if Gillian and Trigger had talked her up so good he couldn't wait.

"He just texted me, saying he'd just seen you and mentioned I should give you a call. Anyway, I know this is really short notice, but I was wondering if you wanted to have dinner or drinks tonight. Call me if you're free. We could meet at Oscar's. Or any other place of your choice. Take care."

"Oh, shit." She pulled up her chair and sat down. She stared at her cell and blinked. Her first thought was hell no.

But her second one surprised her.

She tapped the callback number. Her sister would be so proud.

CHAPTER 2

Darren "Scout" Finch didn't like the sensation of having his heart beat in his throat. It didn't happen all that often. It was one of those things that was reserved for those moments where he truly felt like a fish out of water, and that didn't happen very often.

Not even when he and his Delta Force team were on an unsanctioned op in the middle of nowhere and almost everything had gone wrong. As a matter of fact, he thrived in those situations because he'd been trained to expect the worst.

Blind dates with sexy doctors were not things he had too much experience with, and he couldn't believe that he'd not only called, but that she'd been free this evening.

Sure, he'd been in relationships before, and the

last one had lasted over a year. He'd even uttered the word love, and he'd meant it. Except, not in the forever kind of way because if he had, he would have fought harder to keep her in his life.

But he'd gotten past it and now it was time to move on. The thing was, after Crystal dumped him, he realized he wasn't getting any younger and the idea of having a family was something that he wanted.

So, when Trigger and his wife offered to fix him up with their pediatrician, who also happened to be the doctor to everyone else on Trigger's team and the few men on Scout's team who had kids, Scout jumped at the chance to meet Talullah.

Thankfully, she said yes to the date as well.

He sat at the bar, nursing a vodka soda water with a lime while he waited. He'd picked Oscar's because it was close to where she worked, as well as on his way home from the base. The only reason he lived this far from Fort Hood was because of Crystal. That wasn't entirely true. He didn't do things because someone else wanted him to. However, he'd bought the townhouse with the idea that she'd move in and she did.

For two months.

And for maybe three weeks she was happy. But

she wanted things that he wasn't willing to provide. His family's fortune wasn't his money to spend. There would be times in his future where he would tap into his trust fund, but only when he got married and had kids.

Crystal also wanted him to change and he couldn't do it. He bended for her, but he couldn't give up the career he'd worked and trained so hard for.

For a Friday night, Oscar's wasn't too packed. He'd put his name in at the hostess station, and he was told it would be about a forty-minute wait. He glanced at his watch. He'd been sitting on this stool for at best, ten minutes.

The front door opened and in walked a little piece of heaven.

His heart dropped to his gut. He couldn't take a deep breath. He pounded his chest and tried again.

Nope.

Damn. Talullah was so much prettier in person. She had this funky haircut where it was longer in the front and shorter in the back. The color was hard to explain because it wasn't just one shade, but maybe five different blends of blond and brunette swirled together with a hint of black tucked underneath.

And her eyes.

Holy shit.

He'd never seen anything so blue. They were deep and rich and he wanted to dive right in and swim around. He swallowed. Hard.

Setting his beverage on the bar, he pushed from the stool, but before he could get her attention, another man raced to her side like a dog in heat. Scout stood there for a moment, contemplating what to do.

He wasn't typically a jealous man, but he found himself puffing out his chest.

She made eye contact, then smiled and waved. But it was a little awkward as the man continued to block her entrance into the bar area, while it appeared she tried to excuse herself.

Well, he wasn't about to be cock-blocked on his first date. If they didn't hit it off, then that would be a different story entirely. He asked the couple next to him to hold the two seats while he strolled across the room.

"Hey, Talullah," he said.

"Scout. So sorry to have kept you waiting." She squeezed his biceps, leaning in and kissing his cheek. Her warm lips lingered.

He inhaled sharply, enjoying the fresh watermelon scent of her shampoo.

"It's so good to see you," she said.

"You too." That, he did not expect, but he wasn't about to complain about a beautiful woman giving him a gentle peck. "Our table won't be ready for about a half hour."

"That's okay. I need a drink after the day I've had anyway." She looped her hand into his elbow, her body touching his with a bit more intimacy than one would expect from a blind date. She hung on to him, caressing his arm as if they'd been together for some time.

"I'm sorry. Who are you?" the man asked, giving him the once-over.

"I told you that I had plans," Talullah said. "This is my date—"

"You never mentioned anything about a date," the man said with some disdain. "May I speak to you alone?"

"I'm sorry," she said. "Now is not a good time." She glanced up at Scout and smiled.

All the oxygen in his lungs flew out of his mouth like a pigeon on a mission to return a message.

"It will only take a minute," the man said. "It's important. It's about my daughter."

She squeezed Scout's arm tighter. "I'm not working. So, any medical questions, please call the office tomorrow and speak to the nurse. Unless it's an emergency, which it's not, but if it was, you should call 9-1-1."

"Talullah," the man said in a hushed voice. "It's personal and I only trust you."

"You can call and schedule an appointment in the morning," Talullah said. "Now, if you'll excuse me. Scout and I are on a date. I'll see you later." Talullah practically dragged Scout toward the bar. "Is that where you're sitting?"

"Yes, ma'am."

She chuckled. "Please don't call me that."

"Okay," he said, pulling out the stool and waving down the bartender. "What's your poison?"

"I'll take a glass of their house Chardonnay."

Scout ordered her drink along with an appetizer, since he hadn't had anything to eat since breakfast.

She glanced over her shoulder. When she turned, her jaw was tight and her brow furrowed. She lifted her hand and rested it on his shoulder. "I'm sorry," she whispered. "That had to have been awkward for you."

"I take it he's been bothering you?" He leaned closer, putting his arm around the back of her chair, hoping he wasn't reading the situation wrong. If he was, he might get slapped.

"I went out on one date with him and I knew I shouldn't. Long story short, he doesn't take hints well, and I suck at being mean, though my sister would have been proud of me tonight between the way I handled him at the office and just now. That said, I worry about whatever might be going on with his kid. But if it were a major medical issue, I think his ex-wife would be calling me."

Scout peered over her shoulder. The bar was a complete square in the middle of the room. Kyle sat kitty-corner to them at the far end with another gentleman. He appeared to be engrossed in a conversation, but every few seconds, he shifted his gaze, yet he always kept his focus lower, as if to avoid eye contact.

However, Scout knew when he was being watched.

"I don't have kids, but I have a lot of friends who do and I know if they had any real concerns about them, they would address them immediately."

"I think he's using that because he told me he'd be here—asked me to meet him—and when he saw me, he thought maybe I changed my mind," she said as she lifted her wineglass to her plump rosy lips. She took a long sip and sighed. "I'm so sorry. This is a shitty way to start an evening."

"Is this why you told me we could go somewhere else if I preferred something that I didn't go to on a regular basis?" Scout had suggested Oscar's for many reasons, but one of them was because it was one of his favorite places.

She nodded. "I knew he'd be here, but I didn't think he'd be so aggressive. Sorry, I went right in and acted like we've known each other for a while, but I thought it might drive the point home and get him to leave me alone."

"You do know he's staring at us." Scout tucked her hair behind her ear. It was a bold move, but he told himself he had a part to play and he was going to enjoy every single minute. "I can think of one thing that might make him listen."

She rested her hand on his thigh. "Yeah? What's that?"

He took her chin with his thumb and his forefinger. He needed to remind himself that this was a game with the intention of making sure that Kyle let her be and it wasn't about him making a move. "Do you promise not to get mad at me and hit me or worse?"

The corner of her mouth turned upward into a sexy smile. "Yes. However, kissing me might be over the top, childish, and slightly rude."

"Do you want him to go away?"

Her tongue peeked out and stroked her bottom lip.

He swallowed a groan. He should not be having this much fun at another man's expense. But from the sound of it, Kyle kind of deserved to be put in his place.

"I won't do it if you don't want me to." He glided his hand to the back of her neck. "It's your call, but for the record, I wouldn't mind it."

Her eyelids lowered. "Aren't we supposed to get to know each other a little better before our first kiss?"

"Growing up I had a boat named *Bass Awkward* because if you take the *B* off bass and put it in front of Awkward you have ass backward and my dad always said I tended to do things that way."

"That's cute," she whispered, leaning closer, her breath hot on his skin.

"Tell me to stop."

She said nothing.

He pressed his mouth over hers and a fire ignited in the pit of his belly. His heart thumped in his chest, beating wildly out of control. Deep down, he knew he should pull away, but he couldn't. Or wouldn't. Instead, he deepened the kiss, forgetting he was in the middle of the bar with people watching. He'd never been one for public displays of affection. A quick kiss was one thing, but this went way beyond that and belonged behind closed doors.

She slid her hand along his shoulder and across his biceps, squeezing gently. "Well, now," she said. "You sure know how to kiss."

"Only because you were the recipient." He winked.

"Trigger and Gillian didn't mention you were full of flattery."

Scout chuckled. "Trust me. I'm not. I don't give out compliments freely and a good kiss only becomes a great one when the person on the other end—" He cut his statement short when he realized he was going down a road that could get him into serious trouble. He shouldn't assume she was as into locking lips with him as he had been. That was about as arrogant as he could get. He quickly stole a glance at Kyle who continued to chat with another man. "Let's leave it at we both enjoyed it and I'll add in I hope the date goes well so I can kiss you good-night." Jesus, he sounded like a loser.

He decided that it was that jerk-off that had tossed him off his game.

Or maybe it was the kiss.

"Do you go on many blind dates?" she asked.

"This is only the second one I've ever been on," he admitted. "The first one was a long time ago."

"How did it end?"

"We dated for a couple of months, but I was transferred to a different base, so it ended."

"Does that happen to you a lot?" She scrunched her nose. "I mean do you have to move often? I wasn't asking about how often you're in and out of relationships."

He let out a short laugh. But sadly, the two were somewhat related.

"The Army has moved me a few times, and then because of the training I've wanted to do, like with the Rangers and now with Delta Force, I've had to move. But I'm hoping this is the last one for a long while. I like it here. Not to mention I like the team I'm with. We've really melded well together. We're a family and I like that feeling."

The bartender returned with a platter of sharable appetizers. Scout picked up a loaded potato skin and took a bite.

"That's important." She lifted a mozzarella stick and nibbled on it. "Trigger and Gillian spoke very highly of you."

"They're good people," he said. "They gushed

over you. Told me how great you are with their kids. Trigger has been trying to get me to agree to go out with you for a couple of weeks."

"Weeks?"

He nodded. "He kept telling me every time I saw him at the base that he had an appointment coming up for the twins and that if I didn't agree, I might lose my chance. Finally, when I was at another friend's house for a party, Gillian got in on it and I thought I had to see what all the fuss was and so far, I'm really glad I agreed."

The corners of her mouth tilted into a small smile. "I'll be honest. My first reaction was to say no to this date."

"Do you mind if I ask why?"

"The last relationship I had didn't end well," she said. "And then there's Kyle."

Scout's belly soured. He had a strange feeling that this Kyle person was going to become part of the fabric of this evening whether he liked it or not. What he needed to find out was if she had any feelings for him and she was simply using Scout to make him jealous, or if the guy was just an asshole who didn't know how to read social cues.

"Not that I want to sit and talk about another man, but tell me more about what happened on your date and why Kyle is becoming a problem." Until he had a better handle on the situation, he made sure he kept his arm hoisted over the back of her stool and leaned close.

"He was an issue before I agreed to go out with him." She turned, then quickly snapped her gaze back to Scout. "He's a pharmaceutical rep, so he's in my office on a regular basis. But until recently, he always made an appointment."

"How recent?"

"About three months ago he started showing up to see me without an appointment and not for business. The first two times I made room for him, which threw my entire day off, making patients wait. And it was all for basically a social call."

From the slight tremor in her voice, Scout could tell she wasn't thrilled about any of that.

He wasn't happy about the trauma it caused her, but it meant his night had a fighting chance and a second date had potential.

"When he showed up again, I made him wait until I had a break. I told him that I wouldn't see him unless he had an appointment. That's when he made it about his daughter. I can't get into that, but the next couple of times I saw him either on my lunch or after work. I listened to him, offered advice, but did my best to keep it professional."

"I understand you can't break patient confidentiality, but can you tell me anything about how he framed those visits?"

"He recently went through a divorce. He doesn't have nice things to say about his ex-wife, who I think is lovely, but that doesn't mean they didn't have a crappy relationship. He often used that as part of his ruse to get me to talk with him and how that was affecting his daughter."

"No offense, but isn't that for a psychiatrist?"

She nodded. "I recommended a few colleagues of mine. But he wouldn't give up and at the end of each visit, he'd end it with asking me out. He'd tell me how drawn he was to me and I'd always say no."

"Until you said yes."

She tucked her short hair behind her ear. "When I agreed, I told him that it was one date and that if I thought we didn't hit it off, that would be the end of it and he promised he'd leave me alone. I honestly did everything I could think of to prove we were the most incompatible people, but when he walked me to my door, he wanted to come inside. I obviously said no, and then he tried to kiss me."

"Tried?" Scout was not normally a jealous man.

He believed that if that emotion raised its ugly head, then he was in the wrong relationship.

But right now, he was feeling the pang of it.

"Was he successful?" he asked.

"Nope. I turned my head and all he got was my cheek. I thanked him for dinner and told him that I was not interested."

"Again, I mean no disrespect, but did you use those words?"

"No. I was polite about it and danced around the subject, but I believe I made my point," she admitted. "I'm so sorry. We shouldn't be spending our time talking about this."

"Don't worry about it," Scout said. "Besides, I believe he's leaving."

"Thank God for small favors." She lifted her drink and downed the final gulp. "Please tell me he's not coming over here?"

"Nope. Looks like he's heading right for the door." The hostess waved to Scout. "And our table is ready."

"You still want to have dinner with me after all that drama?"

"The night is still young. Who knows, maybe my ex will make her way in and she can tell you all the reasons I'm a shitty boyfriend."

"You're funny."

He handed the bartender his credit card, closing out his tab. "I have my moments." He stood, pressing his hand on the small of her back as they made their way toward the back of the restaurant and to their table. He tried not to watch her hips sway back and forth, but it was impossible not to notice her toned body.

There wasn't anything he didn't enjoy about Talullah, particularly her honesty. However, when he had a few moments to himself, he would be texting his buddy Lance with Kyle's name so Lance could do a little digging while Scout enjoyed his date.

Because something told him, this night was going to be the start of something special.

CHAPTER 3

Talullah honestly hadn't wanted the night to end. It had gone so much better than she had expected. Especially considering how Kyle nearly ruined it. She stared at her half-empty glass of wine as she nibbled on the chocolate cake they had ordered to share.

She wasn't hungry.

But she didn't want to leave.

Of course, she could use the excuse that she'd had three glasses and it might not be a good idea for her to drive.

Then what?

Invite him in have sex on the first date?

No. She couldn't do that. Well, she could and the thought had crossed her mind. However, this guy was something special. Someone she wanted to bring to Sunday dinner. Those men she never slept with until at least the third or fourth date.

"You are deep in thought over there." He tapped her calf with his foot under the table.

"I've really had a good time tonight." That sounded lame.

"So have I." He set his fork down and wiped his lips with his napkin. "Enough so to do it again?"

She smiled. "I'd like that."

"Tomorrow is Saturday, so I don't have to be at the base. Is it safe to assume you're not working?"

"That would be an accurate supposition."

"Do you have any plans during the day?" he asked.

"Other than laundry and cleaning, which I could put off, I do not."

He laughed. She loved the way it rumbled in his throat and projected across the air, landing in her ears, settling into her muscles, making them twitch with delight.

Scout had a wicked sense of humor, and he certainly didn't take himself too seriously. He was laid-back and he didn't spend the entire night talking about himself.

Something that Kyle had done.

Nor did Scout project his opinions on her, almost expecting her to agree with whatever he was talking about like Kyle did. Scout listened to her and seemed genuinely interested in her life, her past, her career, and anything that tickled her fancy. He'd lean his elbows on the table, resting his chin in his hand, and stare intently. If there was a pause in her speech, he didn't fill it with something about himself. He either waited for her to catch her breath and continue, or he asked an interesting question.

He was fully engaged in the conversation.

But the best part was when it came time for her to probe into his world. He was proud of his accomplishments without being arrogant and rude about it. He didn't spend exuberant amounts of time explaining things. He treated her like the intelligent woman that she was and if she didn't understand, she asked.

He answered. Again, speaking to her, not at or down at her.

Scout was a delight and she wouldn't pass up a chance to spend more time with him.

"I'd like to take you on an adventure of sorts."

"An adventure? What does that entail, precisely?" In the past, she'd immediately say no to something like this, but he intrigued her in ways that made her want to step out of her comfort zone.

"May I surprise you?"

Her heart fluttered up to her throat. She hadn't felt this much excitement since she was a teenager and her father took her and her sister swimming with the dolphins on vacation. It had been one of the most memorable experiences of her life. She often used that as one of her happy places when she found herself in need of a pick-me-up. "Should I be scared? Because I don't like to be scared and I'm generally not a fan of surprises. My sister? She loves them. Demands them. Me? I would rather know exactly what's happening."

"If we get there and you're uncomfortable, we don't have to do it. We can find something else you'd like to do."

She tilted her head. "Is it dangerous?"

"No. But it might frighten some people."

"Now I'm seriously intrigued."

"Is that a yes?" he asked with a bright smile. Beaming actually.

"Yes," she said. "What time should I be ready and what should I wear?"

He downed the last of his beer. "Jeans and a T-shirt should do the trick and how about I pick you up around ten?"

"Sounds like you've got yourself a second date."

"You'll need to text me your address." He waved the waiter over.

"Oh. Let me—"

"I'm not old-fashioned," he said. "Except where first dates are concerned. And second ones. Maybe, if we have a third one, you can pay, or we can go Dutch."

She chuckled. "I'll remember you said that."

The waiter handed him the bill. She waited for him to finish signing the credit card slip before standing. She took the hand he offered and laced her fingers through his, following him through the room and out into the warm Texas air.

"Where's your car?"

"Over there." She pointed to her white SUV parked in the second row from the building. "Where are you?"

"Back there." He nodded behind them. "But I want to make sure you get to your vehicle okay. And steal a kiss."

"You won't have to steal it. I plan on giving it freely."

He laughed.

Once she got to her car, she turned and rested her hands on his shoulders. "I really had a great time."

"So did I." He pressed his lips against her mouth. It was soft at first. Tender.

His hands took her hips firmly, squeezing before gliding along her sides and around to her back. He deepened the kiss, generating more heat than the summer in Texas.

She enjoyed being in his arms. It was an unexpected delight. It was freeing in a way that she'd desired from other men, but never found. It wasn't that she'd been looking for a man to sweep her off her feet. She wanted a partner. Someone to be her equal in every way.

But she also wanted romance. She wanted that feeling of being high up in an air balloon, floating in the sky with just the wind in her hair. She wanted a partner that would treat her with respect, but at the same time acknowledge her womanhood and all that it brought to the table.

It was hard to find a man who would treat her with the same respect and equality while taking her to his bed at the same time.

Part of her wanted to find out if Scout was really that guy.

He palmed her cheek and pulled away.

"Will you do me a favor?" he whispered.

"Sure."

"Text me that you got home safely. And also, I still need your address if I'm going to pick you up in the morning." He ran his thumb across her cheek before dropping his hand and taking a step back.

"I can do both of those things." She turned and tugged at the handle of the driver's door. Slipping behind the steering wheel, she glanced up. "Thank you again for a wonderful night."

"The pleasure was all mine." He gently closed the door.

Two seconds after she hit the button to start the car, he tapped at the glass. She rolled down the window. "Yes?"

"I hate to be the one to tell you this, but you've got a flat." He pointed to the rear tire.

"You've got to be kidding me. These are brand-new tires." She stepped from her car. "I literally got them two days ago."

"The good news is they will be covered under warranty then," Scout said. "Let's pull out your spare and I'll change it for you."

She smacked her forehead with her hand. "Ugh."

"What?"

"The spare is sitting in my garage."

"Do I want to know why?" Scout asked with a slightly amused tone.

"I tend to be a neat freak and was cleaning my car. I didn't get a chance to put it all back together last night when I got distracted by my sister when her family came over. And I forgot to do it this morning."

Scout glanced at his watch. "We have two choices. We can go back to your place, snag the spare, and come back and I can change it. Or I can take you home and I can call a buddy of mine and have this towed to your place and I'll change it in the morning."

"I don't want to put you or any of your friends out."

"You're not." He pulled his cell from his pocket. "One of my neighbors owns a towing company. This is what he, or someone who works for him, does twenty-four seven. It's not that late. I'll text him directly."

"Are you sure?"

He squeezed her forearm. "I'm not going to leave you stranded out here."

"Thank you." She leaned against the hood of her car and let out a slow breath. She glanced around the parking lot and her eyes settled on what she thought was a familiar car. Squinting, she noticed a shadow. "No. It can't be," she whispered.

"What? Is something wrong?" Scout was at her side in a flash.

Taking a couple of steps toward the center of the parking lot, she focused on what appeared to be an image behind the steering wheel. Just then the headlights kicked on and she had to turn her head as bright lights temporarily blinded her vision.

"Jesus," Scout said. "Turn off your brights, buddy."

The car eased out onto the road, heading south.

"I must be seeing things because that looked like Kyle's car, but he left a long time ago."

"Seriously?" Scout moved to the rear of her SUV and knelt, rubbing his hand all around the tire. He took his phone and flicked on the flashlight app. "Are you sure it was him?"

"No," she said honestly. "It was the same kind of car he drives, but it's dark, so I can't be sure if it's the same color or if it was even him in it. I'm probably being paranoid."

"Until we know what happened to this tire, I'm going to be suspicious and you should be too." Scout shut the light off, stood, and tucked his cell into his pocket. "My buddy's sending a tow truck. It should be here in ten minutes. He asked me to send your address so he could give his guy an idea of where he was going."

"Sure. It's 82 SE Hammondsport Way."

"Holy shit," he said. "We're neighbors. Sort of. I live in the townhouses over on Summerset. I take my runs through your neighborhood most mornings. You just moved in about a month ago, right?"

"Should I be worried about you now too?" she asked tongue-in-cheek.

He chuckled. "I run with two of the men on my team who live in the area. One lives two streets from you and the other across the main road in a different neighborhood. Not to mention another buddy just found out the other day his wife is pregnant and is looking in this area." He leaned against her SUV. "I believe you know both Huck and Cannon."

"I also know Cannon's brother," she said. "I hope y'all will tell your other friend about me because I'm still accepting new patients."

"I'm sure Knox already knows." Scout smiled.

"While we wait, do you mind if I ask you something?"

"Not at all."

"Why do you live so far from the base? And those townhouses aren't small. They are all at least three bedrooms and over twenty-four hundred square feet."

"I'll answer that if you answer why you bought such a big house to live in by yourself."

"Deal." She nodded.

"Crystal, my ex-girlfriend, didn't want to live close to the base or in a neighborhood that was all Army personnel. She really didn't like military life much."

"But half this neighbor is all military families."

"I know. And I told her that, but she thought that would somehow be different. And in some cases it is because not many are Delta Force. There are a lot of officers and men and women who aren't being constantly deployed on missions. But still, it's pretty much a military town."

"Did she think she was going to change you by pulling you farther from the base?"

"You nailed it, but she also didn't want to be in the townhouses. She wanted a house, and I wasn't ready to go there for a lot of reasons," he said. "I did care a great deal about her, so I was willing to have a longer commute. It's not that bad. But I wasn't willing to give up my career. Eventually I won't physically be able to do what I'm doing, but until that happens, I've trained too hard and sacrificed too much to give it up."

"I can understand that," she said. "I dated a man once who thought that when I had children I would stop being a doctor."

"Don't you have to spend like eight years in school to do what you do?"

She laughed. "It's four years of undergrad. Then four years of medical school with three years of residency. It's a grueling process."

"I can only imagine."

"So, I'm being incredibly nosy, but did you buy the townhouse together?"

He shook his head. "I bought it and she moved in. She didn't have a lot of money and I didn't want her to dump her savings into it, so we cut a deal that I'd put the money in up front and if we ever got married, we'd pool our money together anyway. She paid for what she could afford around the house. But she moved out about as fast as she moved in."

"Why?"

"I think she believed I'd chase her and I didn't. But she also thought I was more married to my career and to my buddies than her."

"Do you think she was right?" Talullah asked. She found herself wanting to know everything about his past relationships, more notably the ones that were deep and meaningful, and if he was willing to uproot his life for Crystal, she had to have meant something to him.

"No," he said. "Except I wasn't willing to bend for her in ways I should have because even though I hurt when she left, I wasn't heartbroken enough to chase her out the door."

"Your honesty is refreshing."

"I see no reason to lie to you about any of this." He held up his index finger. "However, there are things that I might choose not to be so truthful about."

"Such as?"

"Things about my job. Or when it comes to other people and I don't feel like it's my place to say something."

"Again, that's refreshing," she said. "So, why haven't you moved since Crystal left?"

"I like where I live. I have a few close friends in the neighborhood and ultimately, I'm too lazy to put the place on the market." He arched a brow. "Your turn."

She'd never told anyone all her reasons for buying this house, except her family. They all supported her, though they thought she needed to find a man. She didn't need one, but it wouldn't hurt to have one. "For starters, I was tired of throwing my money away in rent."

"That's fair," he said. "What else?"

This always seemed so difficult for her to explain to people. Whenever she tried to discuss the need to be completely on her own, everyone told her she already had total independence. She'd been on her own since she graduated from medical school and joined this practice. She'd been lucky in so many ways.

However, she wanted a certain kind of life and she hadn't yet been able to fulfill it.

A house of her own was a start.

"I wanted a place I can walk into and feel like me. Something that I could bend and mold and make specifically to meet my wants and needs."

"You wanted a place to call home in the truest sense of the word."

"Exactly." Goosebumps dotted her skin. No one had ever gotten that sentiment. Ever. No matter how many times she'd tried to put it into words, it always came back in some weird pathetic response on how she was trying to impress a man to see how successful she was but that it would backfire because in the end, that was emasculating.

She always called bullshit on that.

She wasn't looking for someone to take care of her.

Nor was she looking to be taken care of.

She wanted a partner.

Who had more of what didn't matter. It was the equality in how they treated each other that mattered. The rest would work itself out.

Or at least in theory that's what she believed a relationship was all about. She'd yet to find anyone who felt the same way.

"You picked a beautiful home," he said. "Though, big for someone all by themselves."

"It sure is and I'm just hoping I keep up with it all. There's a lot I didn't really think about. The previous owners left me the names of their lawn service and all that kind of stuff, but I wanted to do some of it on my own."

"Well, if you ever need a handyman, when I'm not deployed, I'm happy to help."

"I appreciate that."

He pointed to a truck pulling into the parking lot. "Looks like my buddy's guy is here." Scout handed her a set of keys. "My Jeep is the white one at the end of that row. Why don't you go climb inside and I'll take of this."

"Thanks."

He squeezed her shoulder. "On second thought. Drive my Jeep over here. I don't want you sitting in it by yourself. Just in case."

She shivered at the thought someone—or Kyle— might have given her a flat tire on purpose. Kyle was a lot of things, but she didn't think he'd do that. What would he have to gain?

CHAPTER 4

Scout stood in front of his coffee maker, waiting for his extra-tall travel mug to finish filling. He'd spent the night tossing and turning, thinking about two things.

Talullah and the fact she lived in that big house all by herself.

And her flat tire.

The first one he hadn't minded all that much. While Trigger and Gillian had been talking her up for weeks, he hadn't expected her to be so awesome and fun to be around. He liked everything about her and couldn't wait to spend the day in her presence.

However, he did have a couple of concerns that he wasn't sure how to address. He had no right to judge her and how she spent her money. He'd done the unthinkable and googled her and found out her family came from humble beginnings. So, she didn't have a family trust fund and medical school cost a pretty penny.

He sucked in a shallow breath and let it out quickly. This was the kind of thinking that got him in trouble. Not everyone was after him for his money and Talullah was about as genuine as they came.

That brought him to the flat tire.

He couldn't stop thinking about Kyle and if he'd been responsible for the flat.

He took a sip of the bitter brew, ignoring the burn on his tongue. He twisted the top on and headed out the door.

It would take him about fifteen to twenty minutes to walk to Talullah's house and he'd use his time wisely. He tucked his Airbuds into his ears, took his cell from his pocket, and tapped Knox's contact information.

It rang once.

"Good morning, sunshine."

"That's such a weird fucking greeting to give a dude," he said. Although Knox had been handing that one out ever since he found out his wife was with child. The man was the happiest person on the planet, as he should be, but it was starting to get ridiculous. He was beyond a kid in a candy store. He was freaking Willie Wonka.

"Whatever," Knox said. "So, I did some digging on your pal, Kyle Diel."

"He's not my friend."

"Oh, my God. You are in a mood."

Scout squared his shoulders as he took another sip of coffee. He needed some serious caffeine. And enough of it to fill his veins before he landed at Talullah's house. Which is why he chose to walk instead of drive. He'd need to go back to his place and shower after changing her tire anyway. "Sorry," he mumbled.

"You like this girl, don't you?"

"I don't not like her," he said. "But that's not even the point. She was spooked by that guy and to be honest with you, so was I. So, cut to the chase, and tell me what you found."

"Okay. He's been a pharmaceutical rep for three different companies."

"Is that normal? I mean, I've only really had one job and that's been with the Army since I was eighteen."

"From what I've been able to find out, it's a highly

competitive job space, so not uncommon, but he was fired from his first job."

"Do you know why?" Scout asked.

"I'm still researching that. Lucky has a friend that's a private eye and he's going to look into it. The same PI did find out that Elaine, Kyle's ex-wife, filed for divorce, claiming he was overly possessive, controlling, emotionally abusive, and twice used his fists. She had pictures. He denies he ever hit her and said her boyfriend did that to her. That's why he claims they are divorced. There was no proof of an affair and he was never charged with battery. Currently, they share legal custody, but the mother has physical custody. However, he recently filed a petition for that to be changed."

"When did he do that?"

"He sent the paperwork in at the end of the day yesterday. At least the beginning of it. Lucky's friend, Eric, said it was kicked back because he didn't have enough information. He didn't have all the details, but it sounds like he just didn't have a strong enough case. Yet."

"When kids are involved, one should always err on the side of caution, but if a judge tossed it out, it had to have been weak."

"Eric didn't see any of the paperwork, so I can't

speak to it. Plus, I don't understand the law. But I can imagine it's messy."

Scout didn't have a problem bringing this up with Talullah. He understood that she might not be able to comment, but at least she'd know what she was dealing with. "Anything else I should know about this guy?"

"In college he was accused of harassment. The school took the young woman's complaints seriously and investigated as best they could. However, at the end of the day, no formal charges were brought."

Scout would be interested to know what that girl had to say about Kyle. "Do you know what he was accused of exactly?"

"They had been dating and when she broke it off, he wouldn't leave her alone. He did things like send her flowers constantly. Or show up at places when she was out with her friends. What made her call the police was he used his key, that he was supposed to return, to enter her apartment. He waited for her in her bedroom with rose petals covering her bed. A romantic picnic set up in the middle of the floor. And I guess he wasn't wearing much."

"That's a little ballsy," Scout said.

"There's nothing, though, between that incident

and now, other than getting fired. When Eric finds out why, I'll let you know."

"Thanks, man. I gotta go. I'll catch you later."

"Enjoy your date."

The phone went dead.

He tucked it in his back pocket and sipped his coffee as he rounded the corner, heading down Talullah's street. Her home was the fifth one in and had one of the nicest and biggest lots. She had large trees in the front yard, but not too many. Just enough to give her some shade in the hot summer months. Her bushes, which he didn't have any clue as to what they were, blossomed into these bright colorful things every spring.

The house itself was white with a dark brown-gray color with white trim. It had been remolded, he was told, about five years ago. He hadn't ever seen the inside, but he was told everything was brand new and state-of-the-art.

Strolling up the driveway, his pulse increased. The mere idea of seeing Talullah again made his muscles twitch. Last night, he'd wanted to examine the tire more closely, but it was late and he hadn't wanted to spook her more. He was happy to find out she had an alarm system and she'd promised to set it.

They'd shared an epic kiss on her front porch

stoop and even though he thought about pushing the idea of a nightcap, he thought better of it. Not because he didn't want to spend more time with her, but because he couldn't trust himself. He'd put the moves on Crystal pretty fast and he realized he hadn't known her as well as he should have.

A mistake he wouldn't repeat.

He needed to know for sure that his instincts about Talullah were spot-on.

He pressed his finger on the doorbell and turned, staring at her SUV and the flat. He hadn't seen any noticeable marks on the tire.

That could mean a slow leak, which meant it probably wasn't anything nefarious and he was being completely paranoid for no reason. However, he'd still have the tire examined by his buddy at the shop.

The sound of the door creaking open caught his attention.

"Good morning." Talullah stood at the threshold wearing a pair of fitted jeans that stopped about three inches above her ankles. She sported a black sleeveless shirt that hugged her body like a second skin. She pointed to his hand. "I see you brought you own."

He glanced down at the mug in his hand. "Oh. Yeah. But I'll be needing a refill shortly."

"Good. Because I made an entire pot."

"You don't have one of those doohickeys that you put a pod thing in and it makes one cup at a time?"

"Oh. I do. But it also has the capability of making more, so I did."

"That sounds above my pay grade." He laughed.

"Come on in and let's top you off and make you a bagel."

His stomach growled. All he'd scarfed down so far was a banana. "Do you have peanut butter?"

"I think I can manage that." She stepped aside.

"Wow. This is place is amazing." He stood in a two-story foyer that was painted a white-gray color. She had a funky wood bench under the staircase. To the right was a small office which she obviously had barely begun to organize as there were boxes all around her desk.

To the left was a spacious family room that was open to the kitchen, both decorated in a contemporary style with white leather furniture in the main room, complimented by a dark coffee table and end tables. Her artwork was placed against the wall and had yet to be hung.

The kitchen counters had a dark-brown swirl

pattern with specks of blue. The stools around the island picked up the same colors as did the chairs around the table.

Because the space was so open, natural light filled the house, keeping everything bright.

"Thank you. I'm lucky that the previous owners had done so much work. All I have to do is unpack, but that's taking forever."

"I'm happy to help." He climbed up on one of the stools at the large island in the center.

"Be careful what you offer because I might ask you to help me hang stuff."

"Hand me the measuring tape, a hammer, and some nails."

She took his mug from his hands and twisted the cap, pouring more brew. She held up cream and sugar.

He shook his head.

"The fact that you mentioned a measuring tape tells me you might be about as meticulous as I am." After handing him his coffee, she pulled out a toaster from a drawer.

That's when he noticed how bare the counters were and he had to admire that. He couldn't stand clutter. Hated it. Drove him to drink.

"My parents have always been into having this

line up perfectly. When I was little, me and my sister couldn't stand it. We'd tease my mom by walking into a room and moving a lamp. Or leave out the blender. Or worse, make a picture crooked."

"That's mean."

"Now when my folks come visit me, they do the same thing."

"Payback's a bitch," Talullah said. "You didn't mention to me you had a sister. Tell me about her."

Scout's chest tightened. It had been eight months since his sister lost her child shortly after birth. He knew Hannah and her husband, Greg, were trying to get pregnant again, but she barely spoke about it in part because she was afraid. Scout couldn't blame her and he didn't bring it up. She'd tell him when it happened and when she was ready.

He just hoped for her sake she would be able to conceive again, and that this time there were no complications.

Talullah dropped the bagel on the plate and reached across the counter, taking his hand. "Did I say something to upset you?"

He blew out a puff of air. "No. Hannah, my sister, and her husband have been going through some stuff and sometimes when I think about all they've had to deal with, well, it sucker punches me in the gut."

"I hope it's nothing too serious."

"It was pretty bad." His eyes burned with tears that didn't exist. He found himself wanting to share with Talullah and that made him slightly uncomfortable. It was one thing to be attracted to her and to want to get to know her better. Or even to think about her as a potential girlfriend. But this went into deep emotional shit and he wasn't ready to put himself in that position again. Only, he found himself opening his mouth. "They lost a child shortly after it was born. It was devastating to our entire family."

Talullah held his hand tighter and blinked her eyes slowly. "That is a pain I can't even imagine," she whispered. "I've witnessed it in my career, but I don't pretend to comprehend what a parent goes through."

For a second, he'd forgotten she was a pediatrician. "That must be hard for you as a doctor."

"I'm supposed to help heal my patients, but when that doesn't happen, there is always a sense of powerlessness and failure," Talullah said. Her words were laced with thick emotion. Her nose crinkled and a sadness filled her eyes. "Is she older or younger?" She gave his hand a squeeze before turning her attention back to his bagel and peanut butter.

"She's two years younger. We've always been close."

"It's nice to have a sibling to rely on." She placed his food in front of him and leaned on the counter. "My older sister and I are as thick as thieves. I'd be lost without her."

"Hannah and I are the same way, but things changed a little after she lost the baby. I try not to have her be my sounding board on a regular basis, but that sometimes annoys her."

"I'm not a psychiatrist, but I'm sure she doesn't want you to treat her with kid gloves."

"Those were her exact words." He lifted the bagel and took a huge bite. God, he loved peanut butter. He let out an audible moan. "I could live on this shit alone." It wasn't the best way to change direction of the conversation, but he really didn't want to stay on the heavy stuff. Not right now anyway.

"One of my favorites too." She reached out and took the other half of his bagel and took a bite.

"Hey. That's mine."

"Are you telling me you're not going to share?"

The ability to switch between the hard topics and

light and airy wasn't something that everyone could do seamlessly. Most people tripped up on the clunky transition, but not Talullah. She took his social cue and ran with it.

He reached out with his index finger and ran it across her lower lip and chin where some peanut butter had dribbled. He stuck it in his mouth and sucked. "I suppose I can."

He wanted to stand up, stroll to the other side of the counter, press himself between her legs, and kiss the hell out of that mouth. However, he'd wait until later. Good things happened to patient men.

That's what his mother always told him, and he chose to take all that good advice, for a change.

"Why don't we go find that spare tire of yours?" He wiped his hands on a napkin and tossed it to the plate.

"It's in the garage. You'll see it. I think everything is there you will need." She turned and took something off a hook on the wall. "Here are the keys to my SUV. I'll be out in a second."

"Take your time." He took his mug and made his way to the garage where he wanted to die and go to heaven. Not only was it the cleanest garage, but it had a workbench that most men would cut off their right arm for. Only, it didn't have much in it. Thankfully, her spare tire came with a kit and had every-thing he needed. Otherwise, he might be hoofing it back to his place.

He started off by loosening the lug nuts before setting up the jack and lifting the car up. He pulled the tire off and set it to the side.

The hot Texas sun beat down on his back. He wiped the sweat off his brow as he stood. Screw it. He lifted his shirt off his head and tossed it to the side. He snagged the spare and shoved it into place. He worked the tools, tightening everything into place. He wanted to get this part done so that he could focus on the flat.

"Everything okay out here?" Talullah appeared at his side with two bottled waters.

"Was just about to examine the tire." He lowered the jack and wiped his hands with his shirt before taking the cold beverage.

"What the hell are you going to wear home now?"

"My shorts." He glanced down.

She fanned her face. "You're going to give all the ladies in the neighborhood a heart attack walking around like that."

He tossed his head back and let out a hearty laugh. "I'm only concerned about the effect me being shirtless might have on you."

"That depends on if you plan on flexing any of those muscles."

"I feel so used." He lifted the flat and began to exam it for holes, slashes, or nails. He looked at the individual threads, which all seemed fine. Nothing stuck in them that would have caused the tire to deflate. No tears or rips anywhere.

Either there was a slow leak, or someone let the air out on purpose.

It was the latter that worried him.

"If it's okay with you, on our way to our adventure, I want to drop this tire at the shop to have my buddy look at it."

"Is there something wrong?"

"I don't think so. Or at least I can't see anything. But he's the expert. We can pick it up this afternoon if it's something that needs to be dealt with under warranty."

"I really appreciate you doing all this for me."

He wrapped his arms around her waist and heaved her against his chest. "It's my pleasure."

"You're all sweaty." She pressed her hands on his shoulders, but instead of pushing him away, her fingers glided across his skin. Her tongue peeked out between her lips, licking them in a broad stroke.

His pressed his mouth over hers in a tender

kiss. He had every intention of letting it linger for only a few seconds, but instant heat exploded. When he'd agreed to the blind date, he had no expectations. His last relationship had left him wondering if he'd ever find someone who understood not only who he was as a man, but accepted him. While he still had so much to learn about Talullah, he found himself wanting to jump in with both feet.

His mind told him to take it slow, but his hands smoothed down her round ass, cupping at least one cheek, since her cell was tucked in one pocket.

It vibrated, making her jump, cutting off their embrace.

"I'm sorry," she said.

"Don't be. Do you need to get that?"

She stared at her phone with a frown. "No." She tucked it back in her pocket. "Ugh. Mrs. Hawkin is staring. I've only met Judy a couple of times, but she seems like a real busybody."

"She can be," Scout said. "She's nice, but she'll get in your business."

"You know her?" Talullah glanced at her phone and frowned. "She was the first person I met in the neighborhood when she brought me lasagna. She seems like a sweet old lady, but then Trish and her husband next door told me I should be careful when it comes to her."

"Judy knows my ex pretty well," Scout admitted. "Crystal was her nurse when she injured her hip and she's not too fond of me."

"Would that be the same nurse that visits her still today?"

"Yup," he said. "Crystal and I might not have been made for each other, but she's a good person and an excellent nurse. She cares deeply for her patients and always goes the extra mile."

"Maybe for her patients, but she's got a bug up her butt for you."

"You met Crystal?" He arched a brow. "And she was talking about me?"

"I stopped by Judy's house to return her pan and she was visiting with a young woman. They asked me to join them for a glass of wine. Since I didn't know anyone, I thought why the hell not. Now that I recall that meeting, her name was Crystal. They were talking about how she'd run into her ex-boyfriend when she'd been at the grocery store on the way over—"

"I remember that. About three weeks ago?"

Talullah nodded. "She thought you looked good and paid you a compliment and all you did was

grunt and treat her poorly, which she didn't understand because things had been going so well."

"Not exactly what happened," he said. "I was on
the phone with my sister, who was having a difficult
day. Crystal has issues with me and how close I am
to Hannah. She thought it was weird." Scout rubbed
the back of his neck. He'd made a promise to himself
when he and Crystal called it quits that he wouldn't
disparage her to anyone. She didn't deserve that, no
matter what they had gone through, or what she
might have said about him that wasn't true, she still
wasn't a bad person.

Misguided maybe, but not horrible.

"Do you mind if I ask what else she said about
me?" After that run-in, he received a scathing email
from Crystal. It went beyond anything he'd ever
seen from her in the past. Worse than in their last
few weeks together, or in the month they tried to get
back together.

Brutal could be the only way to describe it.

"I honestly didn't stay very long when I realized
it was going to be a bitch session. However, she
talked about how she was tired of the games and
didn't think it was fair that you lived in the house
that the two of you picked out together."

"We might have looked together, but it's in my name, and I paid for it."

"That's fair. She also mentioned how she thought the two of you would be getting back together, but that your family always seemed to get in the way."

Scout pinched the bridge of his nose. "I've spoken to her maybe five times in the last three months and none of them have gone well. And I was never on board to get back together. Not after she walked out the door. Once that happened, I knew it was over. I understood we weren't meant for each other and that was it."

Talullah held up her hands. "Not that it's any of my business, but did she believe there might be a chance when she walked?"

"I'd be shocked if she did," he said. "When she packed up and left, we were done with each other. We went out a couple of times after that, but it was clear we were two people who wanted different things."

"And what did she want?"

"For me to quit Delta Force, get married, and buy a big house on the river. I'm not opposed to marriage, a family, or kids. But she believed that my career isn't compatible with raising children. It didn't matter how many of my buddies I put in front of her that have successful—" He paused, shaking his head. "Why are talking about this?" He also wanted to end the conversation because he didn't want to get into the money aspect of this conversation. He didn't want to go there, and Talullah didn't need to hear. He had no idea if she even knew who he was, though one had to live under a rock not to know what the Finch name stood for. Even if she didn't know, it would be interesting to see what her reaction would be.

His heartbeat raged wildly for a few moments.

He loved his family, but sometimes he hated their station in life.

"Sorry. I tend to ask a lot of questions."

"It's okay. However, for the record, I'm not hung up on my ex."

"You've made that clear." She smiled. "And I believe you. I also believe that Crystal still has feelings for you and is bitter that you let her go without a fight. When she was at Judy's, she kept talking about how once your deployment schedule settled, you'd realize how much you missed her and you'd be begging her to come home, but that she wouldn't until your family understood her boundaries."

"Jesus, that's kind of funny." The more distance he got from his relationship with Crystal, the more he realized how possessive she'd been and how she tried to drive a wedge between him and his family, specifically his sister. She really took offense at how much time he spent talking with Hannah. Besides his career, that had become one of her biggest bones of contention. Especially after Hannah had lost the baby.

Crystal didn't like how often he went home to visit his family. She thought a grown man shouldn't be catering to his baby sister's needs. That it should come from her husband, which it did.

But Crystal didn't understand that Greg struggled too and they both needed all the support they could get.

"What I find interesting is how you manage to have such kind words for Crystal," Talullah said.

He shrugged. "I certainly don't wish her any ill will. I just don't want to have anything to do with her anymore." He glanced over his shoulder. Judy still stood in her front yard, watering her plants, constantly looking in their direction with a scowl. He took his water bottle and unscrewed the top. He smiled.

"What is that grin for?" Talullah asked.

"You look as though you need a little cooling down," he said, waving the bottle around.

"Oh, don't you dare." She backed up.

He lunged forward, spraying her with the water.

She ran off screaming and laughing.

He caught her with his arm, circling it around her taut stomach, tucking her back to his chest. He brushed his mouth across her neck. "I need to go home and shower. I'll be back in forty-five minutes to pick you up." He put a little distance between them because if he didn't, he'd be using all his best moves in hopes of seeing the inside of her bedroom.

She leaned in, kissing his cheek, letting her lips linger for what seemed like an eternity. Her hot breath tickled his skin and crawled across his body like butter melting over an ear of sweet corn. "I'll be waiting with anticipation."

His shower was going to have to be with ice cubes.

CHAPTER 5

Talullah blinked as Scout pulled into a small airfield not far outside of Killeen. "What are we doing here?"

He shifted the gears of his SUV into park and turned. His smile was bigger than a kid after being given a second helping of dessert. "Before I decided to go to Ranger School, I was a test pilot. I don't get to fly that much for the team since someone else is dropping us off and picking us up, so I keep a plane here."

"Don't you have to be like a billionaire to own those?"

He laughed. "I built my plane myself. It's just a small two-seater. It's not a jet or anything like that."

She swallowed. "No offense, but the idea of going up in something you built is a little frightening."

"It's inspected by the Federal Aviation Administration and they have to fly it with me before they will allow it to continue to fly."

"I'm not sure that makes me feel any better."

"Would a helicopter make you more at ease? Because I have one of those here too."

She put her finger in her ear and gave it a good waggle. "Did I hear you correctly?"

"Technically, the chopper belongs to my dad. It's his way of making sure I can get home as quickly as possible whenever necessary."

"Where does your family live?"

"Union Springs, Louisiana."

"That's only about a four-and-a-half-hour drive, right?"

"My mom can be an impatient woman," he said. "More so when I've been deployed for a long time and she hasn't seen me in a while."

"That makes sense." She blew out a short breath. Flying hadn't been something she generally enjoyed. She did it, but it wasn't by choice, only necessity.

"So. Would you rather go up in a small plane or a helicopter?"

"I'm not sure."

He took her hand. "Why don't we take a walk and go check out both, and then you can decide."

She nodded.

"Hey." He leaned across the front seat and took her chin with his thumb and forefinger. "If you're not comfortable, we don't have to go up. I get it. No pressure on my part."

"I appreciate that. But if I let my fears control me, I'd never do anything."

"I like that attitude." He smacked his lips against hers.

She could get used to the way those felt on her mouth. After slipping from the vehicle, she took his hand and followed him through the parking lot toward the gate.

"Look." He pointed toward the runway.

A small plane roared down the pavement.

"That's a friend of mine. Used to be a fighter pilot for the Navy. He was forced into retirement after he was injured in a crash after a serious dog fight about three years ago. I bet his oldest boy is at the helm. He's seventeen and wants to follow in his dad's footsteps."

"How bad were the injuries?"

"He's lucky to be alive," Scout said. "He's got a lot of metal in his body, some serious burns, but as he likes to joke, he's the bionic man and the most important thing is he's vertical."

"How does his wife feel about their son joining the military?"

"I can't say she's totally thrilled with the idea, but she'd never say that out loud. Not in front of Nickolas or her husband." Scout took a stiff stance and saluted the plane as it whizzed by.

A man in the passenger seat did the same in return.

Nearly brought tears to Talullah's eyes.

"It takes a special person to be married to a first responder or a career military person," she said.

He pressed his hand on the center of her back and nudged her toward the big tin buildings on the side of the runway.

Her pulse tickled her gut in a combination of fear and excitement.

"I'm sure it takes a similar person to be in a committed relationship with a doctor between the long hours, being on call, and stuff like that."

"That's true too," she admitted. "The last real boyfriend I had didn't like it when I was on call. I always had to answer my phone, and new parents always call with some silly things and sometimes, to ease their concerns, I would spend some extra time talking with them, or even meet them in the office if they persisted."

"Isn't that what a good doctor does?"

"Not necessarily," she said. "I've had to learn the hard way that some parents are over the top." She tugged her cell from her pocket and waved. "For example, our friend Kyle. He's texted me four times today wanting to discuss a personal matter regarding his daughter. I've turned my phone to silent, except for favorites, so I won't notice it when he does pester me, but tomorrow, starting at seven in the morning, I'll be on call, and if he phones into the call center, I'll have to take it and deal with it."

"Do you have a lot of parents like him?"

"I have a couple who call constantly, but he's the only one who calls my personal line. But that's my fault. I gave it to him and I did go out with him."

"That doesn't give him permission to hound you like this."

She had to agree. "I'm handling it."

He paused at the opening of the hangar and arched a brow. "Are you? Because from where I'm standing, you're too nice to him and certainly not firm enough."

She didn't disagree. "It's a fine line because I work with him and his daughter is a patient. I have to choose my words wisely."

"If it were me, I'd tell him to fuck off." He lowered his chin. "I apologize for my foul mouth."

She sighed. "Sometimes that phrase is necessary and I wish I could use it. Now, which one of these planes is yours?"

"Come on." He took her hand and tugged. "It's the one behind that fancy one over there."

"That red and white one with…" She laughed. "…your name printed on the side."

"Scout isn't my actual name. It's a nickname a friend of the family gave me."

"Why? And what's your real name?"

"Darren," he said. "But the nickname came from the book *To Kill a Mockingbird*."

"Oh, my God. Your last name is Finch. Scout Finch."

He nodded. "I guess my personality was a lot like hers and the neighbors just started calling me Scout and it stuck."

"That's hilarious. But I'm curious, is Darren a family name?"

"Yeah. My full name is Darren Wendell James Finch the Seventh. It's kind of crazy."

"I take it you're expected to name your son that?"

He chuckled. "I wouldn't say I'm expected, but it certainly is implied." He stopped in front of his plane. "However, I have to have one first and before that, I need to find someone who's willing to put up with me and blah, blah, blah."

Not that she judged; however, it seemed like a pretentious thing to name someone so many things and continue the tradition for seven generations. It was also a rich white person's thing to do. Her family wasn't poor by any means, but she had to pay for medical school herself after her parents took care of undergrad. She knew it had been a bit of a struggle, but they insisted. It's what they wanted to do for their girls.

"I'm sorry. I'm going to hate myself for asking, but your family owns a helicopter. You have an incredibly long name that has been carried on for generations. Is your—"

"You really don't recognize the name?"

"Should I?"

"Are you being serious?"

She nodded.

"Come here." He guided her through the maze of planes to the other side of the building. "Maybe this will help." He waved his hand in front of an impressive dark helicopter with the words *The Finch Hotel* written across the side.

"Holy crap," she mumbled. Her cheeks flushed.

It's not like she'd ever stayed at one of their hotels. As if she could have afforded it considering they catered to the wealthier person, though she did have her picture taken in front of one when she'd gone to NYC with her sister a few years ago. "Are you really the heir to The Finch Hotels?"

"Well, me and my sister are." He chuckled. "You really didn't know, did you?"

"I'm sorry. I never put it together. I mean, who would think they'd ever meet anyone who owns a hotel chain."

"That's so refreshing." He leaned against the helicopter. "I've been begging my dad to let me paint over the name. It's embarrassing to be flying around in this thing with my heritage plastered across it. I honestly only offered it up to you because you seemed incredibly nervous about going up in a small aircraft. That I built." He lifted his hands. "Most trustworthy instruments I know."

She bit her finger and glanced over her shoulder. "You're going to think I'm a pretentious bitch, but part of me wants to go up in the bird just to say I rode in The Finch Hotel private helicopter."

He tossed his head back and laughed. "We've got all day. We could do both."

"Really?"

"Sure."

"Only, I have to ask one favor," he said with a serious tone. One that she wasn't used to from him. "Please don't post any pictures of me. Or even the helicopter. I don't have a problem if you show them to close friends and family, but because of my job—"

"I would never." She grabbed his biceps. "Besides not being a fan of social media and only using it professionally, I don't share things without express permission of others."

"Thank you." He tugged her close, wrapping his warms around her waist. "You're a special lady."

"Not really."

"I beg to differ." He kissed her softly.

It sent a warm shiver down her spine. A guttural moan caught in her throat.

"So, today the chopper and tomorrow the small plane?"

"I can't tomorrow because I'm on call, but maybe next weekend?"

"I'll hold you to it," he said. "It will take a few minutes to get the helicopter on the pad outside. There's a picnic bench just on the other side of the hangar door. Why don't you wait for me there?"

"Okay." Talullah made her way outside, pushing her sunglasses over her eyes. She snagged her cell, thankful that Kyle had not texted her again. "Hey Siri, call Loretta." While Talullah wasn't one to brag, she'd already told her about how well the date had gone last night. So, Loretta would be disappointed if Talullah keep this juicy piece of intel to herself.

"Hey, baby sis, what's up?"

"You're not going to believe what I'm about to do," she said, excitement tickling her vocal cords.

"Are we going to play guessing games? Because if we are, I need to warn you that your two little nephews are running wild and won't be letting me talk on the phone long since hubby is at the hospital today."

Talullah laughed. Andrew and Troy were five and two and they were the cutest little buggers ever. But they were also high energy and a complete handful. They were good kids, but oftentimes they gave their parents a good run for their money.

"I'm about to go for a helicopter ride with Scout," she said. "He also built his own plane."

"Is he rich or something?"

"He's not, but his last name is Finch. As in The Finch Hotels."

"No way," her sister said. "Are you kidding me?

SHIELDING TALULLAH (SPECIAL FORCES: OPERATION AL...

You're dating Darren Finch? I've seen photos of him before. He's freaking hot."

"Where have you seen his mug shot? I get the impression he doesn't like his picture taken."

"There's a documentary of the family. He's barely in it, but they mention a son in the military and show an image. Wicked gorgeous is putting it mildly."

"He's a really good kisser too," she said, glancing over her shoulder, grateful Scout wasn't in earshot. The last thing she needed was him listening to her sing his praises in that department. Or in any department for that matter. While he didn't appear to have an inflated ego, she didn't want to feed it. Not this early in whatever was brewing between them. She had no idea if it had staying power, but she certainly wanted to explore more. "Anyway, he's going to be taking me up in the family helicopter shortly."

"You're so lucky," Loretta said. "If you end up keeping this guy for any length of time, my boys would love that."

"I'll be sure to mention it to him if we keep dating for like a month." One thing Talullah did know about Scout was that he was a kind and generous man and he would gladly give her nephews a ride, if

87

she asked. Only she wouldn't put him in that kind of position. Yet.

"Do you like this guy? As in heavy like." Loretta asked.

"I think I do." Talullah struggled to trust her judgment in men. The man she'd been in a relationship with last year couldn't handle her long hours. He hated it when she was on call and was a prisoner to her cell. The gentleman she'd started to date before Kyle mucked it up didn't seem to care about her crazy schedule in part because he was a workaholic himself, which meant they didn't see each often. That didn't help when Kyle started showing up, acting as if he and Talullah were an item. "I'm not ready to go jumping into bed with him or call Mom and Dad, but there is something about Scout that I'm drawn to, besides his good looks."

"What is he like?" her sister asked with a genuine caring tone. Loretta had always been her biggest cheerleader. Growing up, there had never been any competition between them. While they fought like all sisters did, they rarely went to bed mad at each other, and it was never over boys. Their taste in men couldn't be more different. Loretta went for the nerd type. The studious guy who would be willing to actually go on a date to the library.

Talullah preferred a boy with a bit of an attitude. Not a total bad boy. She didn't want to be with anyone who was going to break all the rules, but she didn't mind giving her parents a hard time every once in a while.

"He's really sweet. And funny, but not over the top. Like he doesn't even have to try to make me laugh."

"My goodness, you are a smitten kitten."

Talullah smiled. She really was and couldn't believe how quickly that had happened or how much she hoped whatever was brewing filled the pot full and maybe even required a refill. Or two.

"He's like no one else I've ever met," Talullah admitted. "You have to promise not to tell Mom and Dad or anyone else, though. This is only our second date."

"I won't say a word as long as you keep me posted."

"I will." She glanced over her shoulder and swallowed her breath as her eyes soaked in all of Scout strolling across the pavement. "I've got to go. He's coming this way."

"Enjoy yourself. You deserve this."

Talullah tapped the red button. Her heart hopped to the back of her throat. She stood and stared at this big helicopter that was dragged by a small vehicle. In front of it strolled Scout with his hands stuffed in his pockets in some kind of *Top Gun* moment.

She swallowed.

Hard.

"Are you ready?" he asked, stopping only a foot from her personal space.

The large flying bird rolled past her, taking a right turn. The sun hit the windows, flashing into her eyes.

She blinked. "Oh yeah." The last time she felt this kind of adrenaline had been when she'd gone bungee jumping the day after she found out she passed her first board exam. She'd been scared shitless, but nothing was going to stop her from experiencing that kind of rush. She'd promised herself that if she'd succeeded the first time, that she'd do the one thing she'd been most afraid of.

Heights and falling.

Since then, she'd been hyperfocused on becoming the best doctor she could.

"For the record, I'm terrified of heights. I only fly because I have to, so doing this for shits and giggles is completely out of my comfort zone."

He looped his arm around her shoulders. "It's

always good to move that zone every once in a while. It's how we grow as humans."

"Now you sound like my father."

Scout chuckled. "He's a wise man."

"You're a suck-up and he's not even here." She leaned into Scout and watched as two men adjusted the helicopter, moving it onto a pad that had a big circle on it. "I've never been in a helicopter before."

"And I've never taken anyone up in it for a joy ride. This will be a first for both of us."

She jerked her head. "Are you serious?"

He shrugged. "I take it to go home because it gets me there faster than anything else and a few times I've used it to transport team members or their families for emergencies. But never anything like this."

Her chest tightened. Her muscles tingled with delight. She wanted to wrap her arms and legs around Scout and kiss him until he had no choice but to have his way with her, but she'd save that thought for another moment. Perhaps this evening.

Yes.

Definitely.

There was no point in denying her attraction.

Or her desires.

* * *

"Can you hear me?" Scout adjusted his mic and glanced over at Talullah.

"Loud and clear." She gave him the thumbs-up sign and a big smile.

It made his heart sing. Never in a million years did he ever believe he'd be taking up this machine for a simple ride. He always worried it would bring out a photographer. In the few years he'd lived in Killeen, he'd been able to avoid major incident. Even Crystal understood his desire to be left alone.

And why as a Delta Force solider he needed to have some anonymity, and for the most part she respected it. At least in the public eye.

But not in private and not with her friends. That's where she demanded he flex his *Finch* muscles and spend where he as an individual couldn't really afford.

"What are these things at my feet?" Talullah asked.

"Tork rotors. Don't worry about those, but don't put your feet on them either."

When he'd first met Crystal, she knew exactly who he was and she'd played it cool. As if she didn't care. But deep down she did care about the money and the status his name brought. She wanted that lifestyle and when he wouldn't—and couldn't—provide it, she didn't understand. Just because his family was wealthy, that didn't mean he was, and his father was a real stickler on his children making it on their own.

Sure, Scout's dad bought him extravagant gifts now that he was a grown-ass man who had proven he had what it took to be self-sufficient and didn't need to rely on daddy's money.

And Scout didn't say no when his dad gave him the cash for the plane or bought him a Harley for his birthday. But when it came to taking care of himself, he demanded he do that on his own paycheck. His father respected that and never interfered. His dad only asked that he be allowed to spoil grandchildren, if they ever came to be.

Scout could get on board with that. However, Crystal wanted the big house right away. She wanted to buy something like what Talullah had, or even bigger, and while Scout could afford that even on his own, he didn't believe they were ready for that. He decided a starter home would be best for a first investment.

Crystal didn't understand. For her it all came

down to the fact he was a Finch and could live like one.

And she wanted that lifestyle.

Perhaps more than she wanted him and maybe deep down he knew that and it's why he couldn't totally give her his heart.

He reached across the cockpit and made sure Talullah was strapped in properly. He flipped a few switches and made the whirly bird sign to the men outside.

It took a couple of minutes for the bird to fire up.

He went through all his safety checks. Everything looked good. But one thing was off. His heartbeat. Generally speaking, flying only kicked it up a notch. Right now, it was soaring at new heights. If he wasn't the pilot, he might consider joining the mile high club.

"Okay. Here we go." He pulled back on the throttle and the chopper lifted into the air. "We're going to move toward the runway and take off that way."

"I thought helicopters just go up."

"They do. But we need to accelerate and lift. Plus, the airfield prefers we do it this way."

She stared straight ahead, gripping the sides of the seat.

"Are you okay?" He pushed up and forward, adjusting and angling toward the runway. He inched harder and faster, lifting higher and higher.

"Whoa," she said. "My stomach just went to my head."

"Do you get motion sick?" He hadn't even considered that.

"No. It's nothing like that." Her smile grew wider. "It's more like how adrenaline flows through your body."

"I know that feeling."

She tilted her head, turning her focus out the window. "It's amazing up here and so different from being in an airplane."

"You can't compare this or even my little two-seater with a commercial jet. Completely different beasts." He pointed. "The base is over there. Our neighborhood is southwest of that. I thought it would be fun to fly over your house."

"Really? I'd love that. How low can we get?"

"Between five hundred and one thousand feet."

"That's pretty low." She leaned forward, pressing her hand on the window. "Everything looks so different from this perspective."

"I love it up here," he said. "And I'm so glad you're not scared."

"I was for about the first five seconds of the flight. But not now." She glanced in his direction. "How do you know where you are?"

"Mostly in a helicopter we use what is known as visual flight rules. That's basically having the ability to determine where I am based on position to the ground and water and regular intervals. So, for example, I can use specific landmarks like highways, mountain formations, and things like that."

"But you'd have to know about them first."

He laughed. "Good point, but we also have different types of GPS these days to guide us, but maps are good too."

"And you were a test pilot for the Army? Why did you want to do that?"

"I became fascinated by flying when I was a kid. My dad hired an ex-Navy fighter pilot and I thought he was the most exciting person I had ever met. I bombarded him with questions as often as I could and he was always happy to answer them. My dad jokingly blames him for me joining the Army, and Skip might have had something to do with that decision."

"Did you ever want to follow in your father's footsteps?"

"Nope," Scout said. "I don't have a brain for business."

"What does you dad think about that?" Even though she was asking him all sorts of things about his family life, and was genuinely interested, she kept her focus on the landscape below.

"He never had a problem with it. All he's ever wanted was for his kids to be happy and healthy."

"It's nice that you have that kind of support. I have a good friend whose dad all but demanded his children take over the family business. The pressure pushed her brother across the globe. They aren't close."

"My family is disgustingly close," he admitted. One of the things Crystal liked at first, but then realized wasn't going to work to her advantage when she tried to make his sister her confidant. "We have no secrets and we tell each other everything right down to my mom knows where and who I lost my virginity to."

"Oh, dear Lord. That's a bit much," she said with a slight laugh. "I have to know. Did you tell her?"

"Yes. But not freely. My mom asked a few questions and I couldn't lie. We're a little strange that way."

"I find that endearing."

He inhaled sharply, but his breath got caught in the center of his chest. He'd never met anyone quite like Talullah. While most people said they admired how tight he and his family, especially his sister, were, when it came to the woman he dated, it always ended up being a bone of contention. With Crystal it had been because anytime Crystal tried to confide in Hannah, it always backfired because Hannah felt as though Crystal was trying to put a wedge between her and Scout and Hannah took that personally. She thought it was one thing to try to get close to her, but something entirely different when Crystal wanted Hannah to pick sides.

Hannah would almost always pick Scout's unless he was being a dick.

And then she would rip him a new asshole in front of anyone and everyone. But she'd always have his six.

He tipped the nose of the chopper lower and headed toward the front of their neighborhood.

"Whoa." She curled her fingers around his biceps and stared at him with wide eyes. "Are we going lower on purpose?"

"There's the entrance to the townhouses." He pointed. "I'm the last one at the end of the street."

He checked his surroundings before dipping

even lower and banking to the left, heading closer to her house.

"Oh, my God. Is that my rooftop?"

"It is." He frowned. Crystal's car was still in Judy's driveway. Worse, he was just low enough that he could make out two people sitting in a couple of lawn chairs on the front stoop.

Wonderful.

While he'd taken Crystal up in his plane a couple of times, she wasn't overly fond of flying in anything but a commercial airliner. Most of the times she'd been around his family had been when they'd come to visit him. The one time she'd accompanied him on a family vacation to Colorado, they had flown by charter.

He had never offered to take her on a joy ride in the family chopper, but she had asked once and he cringed.

She would have a field day with the fact he'd taken Talullah.

He should pull up, but instead, he circled around a bit, letting her take in the sights of her hood from the air. He remembered how much he enjoyed it the first time he'd flown like this. He might have only been ten, but he'd never forgotten.

"I can't believe I was even the slightest bit frightened by this."

"I'm glad you're enjoying yourself." He took her over her office and a few other places she asked and points of interest.

They spent a couple of hours in the air before heading back to the small airport.

He landed the bird with little fanfare. He reached across the cockpit and helped her with the headset.

"Thank you so much. That was the most amazing thing ever." She cupped his cheeks and kissed him hard.

A deep groan filled the center of his chest. He'd known this woman for two days and he found himself feeling things that no one else had ever stirred inside him.

Sure, one could call it lust.

Desire.

Passion.

All of those things were true.

But it was so much more, and he wasn't sure how to compartmentalize how fast it was all happening.

His cell rang and it wasn't just any ringtone. It was "Thunderstruck" by AC/DC and that meant his team leader, Cannon.

Fuck.

"I have to take this." He lifted the cell to his ear. "Yo. What's up?"

"We're needed at the base. You've got one hour. Bring your gear."

He closed his eyes for a brief moment. "How long will we be gone? Do you know?"

"You'll be filled in once you get here." The phone went dead.

"What's wrong?" Talullah asked.

"I'm sorry," he said. "We're going to have to cut our date short. Duty calls."

"Are you being deployed?"

"I'm not exactly sure," he admitted. "All I know is that was my team leader and I'm needed at the base. It could mean I'll be sent on a mission. Or it could mean some kind of training exercise. I just won't know until I get there."

"I hate to sound like a crazy girlfriend, but will you be able to text me when you find out?"

"Yes." He palmed her cheek. "I might not be able to give you any details, but you will know if I will be gone for any length of time." He brushed his mouth over her sweet lips. "Did you refer to yourself as my girlfriend?"

"I might have," she whispered. "But I won't hold

you to that definition. We have a lot of getting to know each other left."

"But I like thinking of you that way, especially if I'm going to be sent off on a mission."

"If that's what you need."

"I do."

"Then it's official," she said.

CHAPTER 6

Talullah took the electronic tablet the nurse handed her and scanned through the notes. During her five years working in this office as a pediatrician, she'd only been involved in an abuse case once. As a mandated reporter, she'd been the one who had to call the authorities the moment she suspected the father had been hitting both mother and child.

Last she'd heard, the couple had separated and the father could only see the child under strict supervision, but he was in therapy and getting the help he needed.

That was huge.

Most abusers never try to break the cycle.

Talullah let out a long breath. Her job wasn't to judge. It was to listen to and examine the child.

JEN TALTY

"How long has Kyle and Brittany been here?" she asked Stephanie, the nurse.

"I can't speak for how long they waited in the emergency room, but they've been sitting here for about forty-five minutes."

"Who have they spoken to?"

"Me, the doctor on call, and the police officer over there. But both the patient and father wanted you present."

"What are they claiming happened?"

"That the mother's fiancé was taking inappropriate pictures of the child as well as touching her sexually and having her touch him," the nurse said. "However, the father said there hasn't been any penetration. Mostly her touching the mother's fiancé."

Talullah shivered. She honestly hoped that what she was hearing was all one big misunderstanding or lie.

"Did Brittany do the talking? Or did her father give all the details?"

"He didn't let her speak much. He said she was too traumatized."

"Has anyone called Elaine? Brittany's mother?"

"No. Not yet. The cops will be questioning the fiancé after we conclude here."

Talullah had never met the boyfriend, but she knew Elaine and that woman was a fantastic mother. Attentive and hyperaware of her child's needs. Maybe more so than Kyle.

"All right." She tapped on the screen and handed it back to the nurse. She'd gotten all the vital information she needed. Rounding her shoulders, she turned and took the five steps back to the exam room where Brittany and Kyle were located. Talullah curled her fingers around the curtain. "Brittany? Kyle? It's Doctor Rossi." She pulled the fabric back and held her breath for five seconds.

Brittany sat on the gurney with her knees pulled tight to her chest and her arms wrapped around them. Her eyes were wide.

Talullah wasn't sure if that was fear behind the young girl's big blue pools, or shock. Or perhaps a combination of both.

The young girl wore a hospital gown and there was no visible bruising on Brittany's body.

"Talullah, thank goodness you're here." Kyle jumped up from the chair he'd been sitting in and lunged toward Talullah.

She held out her hand. "It's Doctor Rossi," she corrected him. She needed to keep things on a professional level. Not just because of the situation, but this would be their new normal.

Kyle skidded to a stop. He narrowed his stare, leaning forward a bit. "I think that kind of formality will frighten Brittany even more."

That had to be the most ridiculous thing Talullah had ever heard. And she wasn't about to even entertain the thought, much less acknowledge the fact that he said it.

"I'm going to need a few minutes alone with Brittany," Talullah said. "Why don't you go get a couple of sodas and a snack. The cafeteria isn't too far away."

"I'm not going to leave my—"

Talullah held up her hand. "Mr. Deil. You requested that I come and speak with Brittany. That you didn't want the ER doctor to do it. It has to be without you present. Trust me. I want what's best and I want to get to the bottom of this."

Kyle turned his attention to Brittany. He took her hand. "You remember what I said." He nodded.

"Yes, Daddy."

Brittany was eight years old. Very smart. Intuitive. But she'd always been a bit on the shy side. At least she had been for as long as Talullah had been her doctor. And she'd been more withdrawn since the divorce.

Typical behavior in some cases.

She tended to be more animated around her mother, but there could be a million reasons why.

"I'll be back shortly." Kyle slipped through the curtains.

Tallulah took a few moments to adjust some things around the room and to make sure Kyle wasn't in earshot. Tallulah wanted to find out what he meant by his last words to his daughter; however, she'd have to be careful in how she went about that. "I'm sure you're pretty scared right now."

Brittany nodded her head.

"I'd like to listen to you heart and lungs. Just like we do in the office. Is that okay with you?"

"Yes." Brittany lowered her knees and sat normal on the edge of the bed.

"Can you tell me why your dad brought you here today?"

"Because of what Jim did." Brittany kept her eyes closed the entire time. Her voice trembled.

"What did Jim do and when?"

"My dad said I don't have to repeat it. That he'll do it for me."

Tallulah pressed her stethoscope against the girl's

back. It was a mere formality, but it also gave her a chance to examine Brittany's body. So far, no bruising or anything that looked suspicious. But if the sexual assault wasn't violent, there might not be.

"In order for us to understand what happened, we need to hear it from you. Only you. And without your parents here." Talullah pulled a chair up and took Brittany's hand. "I know this is hard. But we've known each other a while now and you can trust me with the truth."

Brittany lowered her head and sobbed. "No. I can't. I can't tell anyone."

This had to be the worst part of Talullah's job. "Sweetheart. If you don't tell me, other people are going to come in here and ask you the same questions and they won't let your father speak for you. Why not do it with me when no one else is around."

Brittany sniffled. "Because I don't know the proper words to use."

"You don't need them."

"But my dad said without them Jim wouldn't be punished."

"That's not true." Talullah squeezed the little girl's hand. "All we need to know is what happened that made you come to the hospital. In your own words because those are the best. It will make it easier for me to understand. Can you do that for me?"

Tears rolled down Brittany's cheeks. She swiped at her face. "It's too hard. I need my daddy."

"How about if you answer a few questions. I'll make them easy. Just yes or no." Talullah stood. "Did you spend the night at your dad's or did he pick you up this morning?"

"He picked me up for breakfast."

Currently, it was two in the afternoon on Sunday.

"And you told him what happened then?"

She nodded.

"Was one of the things you told your father that Jim touches you?"

Brittany covered her face. "I don't want to do this."

Just then, Kyle came bursting through the curtain. "I told you, baby. You don't have to. I'll speak for you." He set the sodas and candy that were in his hands on the tray by the bed before wrapping his arms around Brittany. "What the heck are you doing? I thought I could trust you."

"You can," Talullah said. "May I speak with you for a moment in the hallway."

"Sure." Kyle kissed Brittany on the forehead. "I'll be right outside. Don't you worry. Daddy's here."

Talullah stuffed her hands in her white coat pockets and stepped into the hallway. She faced Kyle. "I know you believe you're protecting her, but you're only making this harder for both her and any chance of building a case if all this is true."

"If? That bastard hurt my baby. You think I'm going to—"

"Please calm down," she said. "The examination shows no injuries."

"Like I told the other doctor, he has her do all the —Jesus, even I struggle to say it."

"Kyle. A social worker and a police officer are going to have to take her statement. And you're not going to be allowed to say a single word. The more you coach her, the less she will be believed. Now, I can sit with her during that process and am happy to do so. However, I would appreciate it if you helped her understand that she needs to tell the truth about what happened to her in order for it to end."

"Okay. Give me a minute alone with her."

"I think it's best if I'm with you." Talullah had been told early on in medical school to learn to trust her gut instincts and her gut told her that something about this entire scene didn't feel right. She hated not believing a little girl, but Kyle's behavior made the hair on the back of her neck stand straight up on end.

"Why?"

"So she gets used to the idea of me being with her when the social worker gets here." Talullah glanced at her watch. "Which will be shortly." However, the real answer had been because she didn't want to give him any opportunity to coach the child.

This was going to be a long day.

* * *

Talullah stepped from the social worker's office. Officer Andie McGee followed.

"There are many inconsistencies in her story," Andie said. "It has changed a bit from when I first spoke to her."

"She's a child and she's scared," Talullah interjected. "However, I do agree. There are some areas of concern when it comes to the way she pieces together what happened."

"Her timeline is off," Alice Gibbs, the social worker, said. "Unfortunately, that's not entirely uncommon. But what concerns me the most is how flustered she got when she went off script. She was definitely coached. I'm going to need some time with her to get her to open up to what really happened."

"I've seen this a few times in custody cases. I don't ever want to see a kid abused, but asking a kid to lie about it seems almost as bad."

"I agree," Talullah said. "Thank you for your help."

The officer nodded and headed toward the elevators.

Talullah let out long sigh. "I don't believe Brittany was sexually assaulted at all." She quickly peered into the waiting room where Brittany played with some dolls on the floor with the receptionist. The poor little girl had been terrified during most of the session.

"She didn't really tell us much of anything. She only implied a few things and repeated word for word what her father told us," Alice said. "And he certainly gave us an earful. But even his account of what she told him seemed off. Maybe you can talk to him again and see if he trips up."

"That's not a good idea." Talullah didn't want to get into her personal life with a colleague, but in this case, she was left with no choice. "I went on one date with the father and to be honest, it didn't end well.

I've been trying to get him to understand there will be no second date. He's quite persistent."

"You mentioned that he wanted to discuss something about his daughter but you ignored him. Is that because of this personal issue?" Alice asked.

"Yes. And he wouldn't give me details about the situation. I thought he was using Brittany to get my attention."

"That very well could be, considering he told the police that he called them as soon as Brittany told him what happened and that he drove straight to the ER," Alice said. "I can understand why you want to take a step back and I agree, under the circumstances, it's a good idea. But I'd ask you to do me one favor."

"What's that?"

"Ask him about why he wanted to speak with you and let me know what you find out. In the meantime, I've called the mom and I will interview her as well as the boyfriend," Alice said. "I read up on the divorce the child's parents are going through. It seems the father accused the mother of a few things that could never be proven, which led to joint custody."

Talullah tried to keep her nose out of that divorce. Kyle had mentioned the affair, but others said his ex-wife never had one. It wasn't any of Talullah's business. Of course, there was all this chatter about how Elaine had been trying to poison their daughter against Kyle.

Could this be payback?

That would really be about the lowest thing a father could do to their daughter outside of abusing her himself. "It was an ugly divorce from what I can remember."

"Did you notice the way Brittany responded when I asked her about lying and the different types of lies?"

"I did," Talullah said. "I thought it most telling when she started asking questions about when someone of authority told you to lie because it was the right thing to do."

"The question I have there is why would it be the right thing? I wonder if he's playing on her emotions about her parents possibly getting back together, or he's painting Jim out to be the kind of man who would take her mother away," Alice said.

"There is no medical evidence that she was assaulted in any way, shape, or form. We only have the father's account of what he relayed back."

"The cops will ask Jim some questions, and then I will as well. Unless something drastic changes and we get some proof of some kind, Jim will walk away and custody will remain the same." Alice held up her finger. "Which reminds me. The father had filed for full custody, but some of the paperwork wasn't correct, so it won't go through until Monday."

This was not a fight Talullah wanted anything to do with. Right now, all she desired was a long hot bath. But that wouldn't happen until tomorrow night after work. She let out a long breath. "Thanks for your time. I appreciate everything you're doing for my patient."

"I'll take good care of her. Don't you worry. And don't forget about my little favor."

"I'll see what I can do." Talullah made her way toward the elevators. Thankfully her office wasn't that far from the hospital. She stepped into the moving box without looking up, regretting that decision the moment she lifted her gaze. She blinked. Shit. She didn't want to do this now.

"How did things go?" Kyle asked.

"You can speak to the social worker about the details," she said.

"I'm asking you." Kyle furrowed his brow. "Why are you being so cold? I need you right now."

The elevator doors closed, locking her inside with Kyle.

"I'm being professional," she said. "I need to ask you a question."

"Okay." He folded his arms in a defensive and closed demeanor.

"You kept texting me yesterday about wanting to speak to me about Brittany. What was that all about?"

He cocked his head. "I've been concerned for her safety for a while now. I wanted your advice on how to proceed."

"Are you saying you suspected she was being abused?"

"Her personality had been changing and I've been concerned ever since my ex-wife started dating that Jim guy. This was exactly the kind of thing I was worried about and wanted to discuss with you, but you didn't give me the time of day." He rubbed his hand over his face. "I'm not blaming you. I'm just very upset and everyone around here is pushing me to the side." He banged at the elevator button. "I should be with my daughter and you and that social worker along with the police keep separating me. I don't like that. Why are you doing that to me? Why won't you talk to me? You and I have always been close. We've always had a connection."

"You're putting me in an incredibly uncomfortable position. I don't mean to be rude, but I need to make myself very clear. I'm so sorry for what is happening right now. However, we are not friends. I'm your daughter's pediatrician. Focus on your family right now and making all this right."

"Making it right? What the hell is that supposed to mean? That asshole hurt my baby. I'm going to make sure he rots in hell. What I don't understand is why you're acting as if I'm the criminal."

"I'm not doing that," she said softly. "I'm setting bound—"

"Brittany needs us on her side. She needs to know that we believe her and will do whatever—"

"Kyle," Talullah said firmly. "Brittany is my only concern and she's in good hands with the social worker."

"I don't understand why the police didn't go straight to Jim's house and arrest him." He reached out and took her forearm in a tight grip.

She jerked her shoulder.

The elevator doors swung open.

"I need to go," she said. "Brittany is down the hall. Third office on the right. Oh, and Kyle. I'm going to give you one piece of advice. Please, whatever you do, don't coach your daughter on what to say."

"I would never." Kyle stepped into the hallway.

She lowered her chin. "It shows, and in the end, the only person you're hurting is her." She exhaled as the doors closed once again. She pushed the button to the lobby and leaned against the hard, cold metal wall. Her intuition had told her that Kyle didn't have his shit together. That there was something just a little off-center about the man.

Well, she was more than right in her assessment.

Only, she'd fed the beast and now she had to pay the piper.

Going on a date with him had to be one of the biggest mistakes she'd ever made.

She flattened her hand across her stomach and closed her eyes.

Scout.

He was no mistake. He was the real deal. Nothing fake or off about that man. He was about as genuine as they came, and she wanted to know everything there was to know.

The good.

The bad.

And everything in between.

As if on cue her phone vibrated.

She pulled her cell from her purse and smiled.

Scout: *I won't be able to reach you after this text. We'll be in briefing and then on a mission that shouldn't,* *if all goes well, last more than 24-48 hours. I will text you as soon as I can. My buddy said if you bring your car in on Monday, he'll put on your tire. It's all fixed.*

Wonderful.

Talullah: *Thanks. Be safe. I'll be thinking about you.*

The text went undelivered.

Bummer.

She'd never dated anyone in the military before. But she'd gotten to know a lot of military families and every single one of them confided in her how difficult it was to deal with deployments. It didn't matter how long or how short; they weren't easy.

And now she was going to experience it firsthand.

Perhaps this would be the kind of test she needed to know if she had what it took to be in a relationship with someone like Scout.

CHAPTER 7

It had been two days and still no word from Scout. He'd told her twenty-four to forty-eight hours and that had passed.

She shouldn't be worried.

She was about to snag a glass of wine, a snack, and bring it to the back patio when the doorbell rang. Racing through the house, she hoped Scout decided to surprise her instead of texting.

But that thought was tossed out the window when she opened the door and Crystal stood on the other side.

"I'm sorry to brother you," Crystal said. "You don't know who I am, but—"

"You're Crystal. Scout's ex-girlfriend."

Shit. Between the bullcrap between what was

going on with Kyle and his daughter, which was still giving her a headache, and now Elaine was bending her ear, this was the last thing Talullah needed.

But at least it wasn't Kyle. He'd texted her a couple of times since the incident at the hospital and she'd responded yesterday telling him that she couldn't have any contact with him outside of medical visits with Brittany. That it was unprofessional of her to have any contact and it would not be perceived well for anyone, especially him. It was a bit over the top and dramatic. But he'd stopped texting her and that had been the point.

"What can I do for you?" she asked.

"I'd like a moment of your time."

Talullah rubbed the back of her neck. "What for?"

"Please. May I come in?"

"How about if I come outside." Talullah had placed two small chairs on the front porch. She waved her hand before closing the door and taking a seat. "I don't have much time, so please, tell me what's on your mind."

Crystal slowly sank into the seat. She stiffened her spine and crossed her legs.

Just as slowly.

It was fucking annoying.

She shook her leg, wiggling her cute little sandal

pumps. Her toes were perfectly manicured, which Talullah found odd for an RN.

"Scout tells me you're a nurse."

"I am," she said. "But that's not what I want to be forever."

"What is it that you'd rather be doing?"

"My career is not why I'm here." There was a fair amount of venom laced in Crystal's words. "I saw that Scout had his family helicopter out the day I saw you and him leave here together."

What the hell were they in, the third grade?

"Okay," Talullah said because there was nothing else to say.

"Scout doesn't like to take it out for joy rides, so how or why you managed that is somewhat of a mystery to me." She held up her hand as if to hush Talullah. "Scout and I have had some problems lately, but make no mistake, he and I are not over."

Oh, dear Lord. A chest pounding, territorial bitch. If Talullah didn't like Scout so much, she'd walk away. But that wasn't going to happen. For the first time since she'd graduated from medical school, she'd found a man that more than tickled her fancy. She wanted to explore all that it could be, but she didn't want the drama.

"That's what you came here to tell me?"

"I'm not sure what Scout has told you about us or about his family. However, I decided a little while ago that I needed a break while he got his head screwed on straight." She waved her hand. "To make a very long story short, his family suffered a great tragedy and it changed Scout and his relationship with his sister. It's on the mend now, but I didn't want to stand in the way of that, so I moved out of our home. But I plan on moving back in within the next few weeks, so I don't want you to get the wrong impression about the ride. It was all for show to make me jealous. Now, it didn't work because I know what and why Scout does everything. But I'm going to let him believe it."

Talullah wanted to bust out laughing. She literally couldn't believe her ears. One thing she'd learned over the years was not to argue with crazy.

And this was about as insane as it got.

"Well, thank you for stopping by." She stood.

"So, you're going to back off."

"I didn't say that, and Scout isn't a chicken bone for us to tug at and make a wish over. He's a grown man who makes his own decisions. So, I'm not going to hang out on my own front porch and even entertain this conversation with his ex-girlfriend."

"I'm not his ex."

This woman was totally delusional. She should introduce her to Kyle. They'd make for a great fucked-up relationship.

Jesus. That would not be good.

"You go on and keep believing that. I, on the other hand, am going to go and crack open a really nice bottle of wine and enjoy my night." Talullah waltzed right into her home and slammed the door. She leaned against the door and blew out a long breath.

Her cell rang.

She raced into the kitchen and found her purse, snagging the phone.

Gillian.

"Hello?"

"Hey, girlfriend," Gillian said. "What are you up to this evening?"

Talullah made a beeline for the bar. She opened the wine cooler, pulled out her favorite bottle of white, and poured a hearty glass. "I'm going to kick back, drink, and forget about why I'm so annoyed right now."

"Would you like some company?"

"Where's Trigger?"

"Same place that Scout is and I happen to have a babysitter, so are you game?"

"Come on over."

"I'll bring the cookies."

Talullah laughed as she tapped the red button, hanging up the call. She knew for a fact that Gillian had a sweet tooth and she wouldn't go back on her word. She quickly texted her to come around to the back patio. It shouldn't take Gillian more than ten minutes to make it to Talullah's house considering they lived only a few neighborhoods over.

While she didn't make it a habit of becoming too friendly with her patients' parents, she'd make an exception in this case. She genuinely enjoyed Gillian's company. They had gotten coffee or juice a few times after exercise class and they had a fair amount in common.

They both enjoyed the same types of books and watched the same shows. While Talullah had tried not to allow her practice to rub off on her personal life, she decided to make an exception in this case. Gillian was good people and Talullah wanted to spend more time with her in general. Even if things didn't work out with Scout. She'd spent so much time working on becoming a doctor that she'd let all her close personal friendships fall through the cracks. All her girlfriends from high school had either left town or she had grown apart from them.

Her friends from college she'd lost touch with and those she'd known in medical school had scattered all over the country and were working on their careers, just like she was.

Being a driven person made it hard to have close relationships; in particular, it made it difficult for her to develop friendships with other women.

That had always been a laborious endeavor for Talullah. She thought it might be because she'd always been so focused. Her sister told her it was because others were jealous.

But Talullah could never understand why.

She wasn't any more pretty than the next girl. Or smarter. If anything, Talullah was average in both categories. Except for in the latter, she worked really fucking hard to make the grade in school and to be successful in her career.

But Loretta always told her that other girls were envious. That they saw Talullah as public enemy number one. That she was prettier and smarter than everyone else in the room.

She never saw it. Never believed it.

But she always ended up with fewer friends.

She told herself that it was okay. That she didn't need them. That she was an introvert and preferred to be by herself, but the reality was she needed people just as much as the next person, but that she hadn't found her people yet. She wanted to laugh at herself over that thought. That statement was only partially true. Part of the problem was that Talullah could be a tough cookie. She accepted the fact that while she wasn't overly judgmental, she did make some judgments.

She took her favorite bottle, put it on ice, and brought it to the backyard. Easing into one of the lounge chairs, she crossed her ankles and lifted her glass to her lips.

God, that wine was good. Cold, crisp, and tasted like a nice cool pear.

She glanced up. The sun had disappeared and the moon hung high. The stars began to speckle the sky, casting a warm glow over her yard. She let her shoulders and every muscle in her body relax, something she hadn't let happen since Sunday. It had been a difficult two days. She'd spoken to the police, twice.

Nothing had ever come of the allegations Kyle and his daughter made against Elaine's boyfriend.

Which Talullah struggled with for Brittany. The poor child had been coached and she would forever be scarred by that trauma. So far, nothing had been proven one way or the other, with one exception.

There was no physical proof that anything had happened.

And Kyle's story didn't make sense compared to what his daughter told when he wasn't around. Talullah had done her best to avoid the man; however, his daughter was important to her and she would do whatever it took to ensure she was well taken care of.

Right now, she wasn't sure what that meant other than making sure the truth was spoken. How Talullah could help would be to support Brittany, and only Brittany. She would have to see Kyle or Elaine—depending on who brought the child in for a medical visit—but outside of that, her contact with the parents would be minimal.

She hoped.

"Hello? Talullah? Are you back here?"

"I sure am. And with a bottle of wine and glass ready and waiting." Talullah turned, looking over her shoulder. "Welcome."

Gillian carried a paper plate. "I have home-baked chocolate chip cookies."

Talullah set the cookies on the table. "Sounds fabulous." She poured a second glass and topped off her own. "I didn't think Trigger and Scout were on the same team. How did they end up on the same mission?"

"The two teams do a lot of training together and oftentimes, on short deployments, they end up working together."

"I thought this one was going to be one to two days. Not that I have a right to complain. We've been on exactly two dates and the second one was cut short when he was called away. Do you know anything about where they went or why?"

Gillian took a long slow slip of wine before settling back in the lounge chair. "Nope. But I saw a C-130 transport return to the base about an hour ago. They always have to debrief before they can contact wives or girlfriends and that can take hours depending on how things went down. I suspect we'll be hearing from them by morning."

"I probably shouldn't ask, but I'm insanely curious. Why did you reach out tonight?"

"Well, first, Trigger and I were supposed to have a date night, and I just never canceled the babysitter, so I thought it might be nice to get to know you better. And second, I heard that Scout took out his family helicopter. That never happens. I wanted the scoop." Gillian turned. She held her glass close to her pursed lips.

Talullah sucked in a shallow breath. "How'd you hear that?"

"I'm not sure I want to tell you."

"If you don't, you can forget about hearing the details." Talullah lowered her chin and lifted a brow.

"His ex-girlfriend goes to the same salon as I do and she didn't know I was sitting around the corner when she was blabbing her mouth about it, but I only want to know what happened from your perspective. Because seriously, Scout doesn't like to toss his family name or clout around. He's only taken that up for emergencies or to go home."

Talullah rubbed the back of her neck. She hated gossip and worse, she despised being the center of it. "Was I mentioned at the salon?"

"Not by name. All she said was how Scout was trying to make her jealous, which is total bullshit. But anyway, what the hell, Talullah. He took you up in the family chopper. He doesn't do shit like that."

"Imagine my surprise when I learned who he was," Talullah said. "Why didn't you tell me?"

"Scout certainly isn't embarrassed by his family. He's so ridiculously close to them it's almost gross. The problem is he's had women want him just because of his money."

"I'm sure that's true of friends as well." Talullah

had some wealthy friends in medical school and she'd seen it all when it came to the way they'd been treated and used by their inner circle. It drove Talullah batshit crazy. She couldn't believe that these people allowed it to happen. "I had a classmate who had so much money that she said it was easier to let people be her fake friend up front than pretend to actually like her while using her for her money."

"That's sad."

"She said it weeded out the people who eventually would like her for who she was and not what she could buy them."

"I guess that would work." Gillian stretched out her legs and crossed her ankles. She raised the wineglass to her lips and sipped. "So, tell me. Have you gone to bed with him yet?"

"No." Talullah's cheeks heated. "But we probably would have had he not gotten called away."

"I knew the two of you would be perfect for each other." Gillian turned and smiled. "He's a good man."

"I can't find anything wrong with him." Talullah fiddled with the stem of her glass. "Tell me something ugly."

"Why would I do that?" Gillian's voice went up an octave.

"Because right now, he's too good to be true and

I'm going to talk myself out of seeing him the second he comes back unless I know he has a flaw outside of the occasional bad taste in women."

Gillian laughed. "He's typical of everyone in Delta Force. He's dedicated to his job. Married to it actually. Not in a bad way, but it does often affect his ability to maintain relationships. In Scout's case, it could be more because he's waiting for whoever he's dating to show her true colors."

"What does that mean?"

"With Crystal, her need for his money and status happened slowly. The sad part is—and you're not going to want to hear this—but they cared for each other. She just couldn't get past the idea he not only doesn't have his parents' money, but what he does have, he's not interested in flaunting."

"You know, coming from someone who lived in a shoebox during my residency, I know that I could never go back to that. Or at the very least, it would be hard." Talullah waved her hand toward her house. She'd worked hard as hell to be able to afford a place like this and she'd be the first one to admit, she wanted more. "Kudos to Scout for downsizing his lifestyle."

"He's a humble man, but I think bootcamp and

the military helped him with that transition from spoiled rich kid to the man you're seeing now."

Talullah nodded. She could understand how that kind of training could reshape a person.

"Trigger is going to kill me for telling you this." Gillian swung her legs to the side. "The thing with Scout is that he's always waiting for the other shoe to fall and when it comes to relationships, he often sets up little traps regarding money."

"What does that mean?" The one thing Talullah hated more than gossip was games.

They were the ugliest when played by grown-ass men.

"You can't blame the man. Women have claimed to have cared deeply for him when they only cared about the status. The red carpet. Or whatever they thought they were going to get being his wife. Especially when he retires. I doubt that will be anytime soon, but it happens to the best of them. And he could end up working for his dad. But at the very least, he and his sister are going to inherit quite the hotel empire."

Talullah hadn't given his family's money a second thought. Or what he might have in the future. It stunned her for two seconds that his family owned The Finch Hotels. After that, he was just Scout. The same man she'd gone to dinner with the night before.

"Scout wants to be with someone who doesn't care about his money."

"While it might not be the money someone cares about, it will be part of the equation no matter what," Talullah said. That fact that he could be a millionaire or billionaire wasn't sitting front and center in her mind, but that didn't mean it wouldn't be part of her thinking in general. If she continued to date him, she knew without a shadow of a doubt his name—his family name—would be part of how she viewed who he was as a man.

Just like people changed their perspective when they found out she was a doctor. Or that she lived alone in a house made for a family.

"What does that mean, exactly?"

"He can't change where or who he comes from," Talullah said. "And since he's close to his family, that makes him tied to it even more. He's not looking for someone to not care. He's looking for someone who respects his choices and loves him because he's a man of honor. But it's hard to attract anything but a bee when you're made of honey."

"Wow. Aren't you the little philosopher."

"I have my moments," Talullah said.

"Maybe he took you up in the family bird because he senses you're that girl."

"I hope it wasn't one of those tests you were just talking about," Talullah said. "Because that is a total turnoff."

"Are you telling me you don't have any trip-up questions for men when you're out on a first or second date? Or that you don't search for certain traits or undesirable characteristics that you'd rather not ever deal with because of past experiences?"

Talullah glanced to the sky, as if the moon and the stars had the answer she was looking for. "Well, when you put it that way, I suppose I do. But you made it sound like Scout tries to catch people in lies and that he trusts no one."

"He doesn't trust easily and it's more about universal core truths," Gillian said.

"Crystal must have hurt him more than he lets on."

"He did care a great deal about her, but she's not the reason he's like this. It started long before her, though maybe he wished he'd seen the signs with her before they began cohabitation."

"What do you know about his girlfriends before Crystal?" Talullah asked.

"Nothing. I've never met any other than Crystal.

But since you want to know some of his flaws, I will tell you that he does place too much value on being frugal. He can't stand it when someone—no, a woman he's dating—wants something for the sake of wanting it and no other reason. But if someone else desires it, he doesn't have a problem. It's worse when the person knows who he is and I've only seen this a couple of times when he's gone out with a couple of girls before and after Crystal. He's very sensitive when it comes to other people's relationship with money."

Talullah wondered if when she didn't insist on paying half on their first date if that had been a test. If so, she failed, but he must have given her a second chance. Or perhaps he was okay with paying for dinner one time.

Shit.

She wished she hadn't known this ugly side. But she asked, so she had no one to blame but herself.

Gillian shifted, pulling her phone from her pocket. She glanced at it and smiled. "I got a text from Trigger. They've been released from the debriefing room and he's headed home." She stood. "I'm sorry. But I'm going to go see my husband."

"Oh. Please. No need to apologize to me."

Talullah swallowed. She didn't have the courage to look at her cell. "Enjoy your night."

"I plan on it." She pointed to the small patio table. "Your screen is lighting up."

Talullah clutched her chest. Her heart squeezed. She stared at the electronic communication device. Part of her wanted to ignore it. If it was Scout, she'd tell him that she'd already gone to bed and sorry she'd missed it.

But she'd have to ask Gillian to lie and that she'd never do. To anyone.

With a shaky hand, she lifted her cell.

Scout: *Hey. I'm back. Sorry it was longer and I couldn't contact you. If you're up and would like a night-cap, I'd love to see you. I'm about to head home. Let me know.*

She wiggled her fingers. Her pulse hammered through her veins like an out-of-control windstorm ripping through the treetops, tearing off the branches left and right.

What the hell.

Tallullah: *Come on over.*

CHAPTER 8

Scout slipped from behind the steering wheel of his Jeep. His heart jumped from the center of his gut to his throat where it pounded in this wild beat. The second he boarded that transport plane, his mind had shifted from the mission to Talullah.

Now that he'd pulled into her driveway, he'd turned into a skittish teenager with no game.

He didn't expect to be invited to stay the night, though he wouldn't be opposed to the idea. However, he needed to make sure she was okay. He'd had this unsettling thought for the entire mission about what had transpired with Kyle.

And then there was the crazy texts he'd gotten from Crystal when he'd landed. She'd informed him that Judy told her that Talullah had been bragging to everyone in the neighborhood about the joy ride he'd taken her on in the family helicopter.

She stood in the doorway. She waved and smiled.

No way would she go around telling people that. If she had, someone he knew from the base would have heard and it would have made its way back to him. This was all Crystal stirring up trouble, trying to win him back with her stupid games.

They were over. And what she failed to understand was that it wasn't about all the things they used to fight over, but he didn't love her anymore. If ever. She needed to accept that and move on.

Only, he couldn't waste his breath explaining it anymore. He'd done it a million times. His best bet was to ignore it.

"Boy, are you a sight for sore eyes." He moved a little faster. Any trepidation he had for reaching out to her disappeared as she opened the door and let him enter. "Sorry it's so late, but I'm so happy you answered."

"I'm glad you texted." She rested her hands on his shoulders and tilted her head. "I was honestly worried about you. I hope things went well with your mission."

"About all I can say is that it was successful." He took her by the hips, easing his hands under her shirt, letting his thumbs circle gently on her soft, silky skin. "And you made the boring moments more bearable."

"There are parts of a mission that aren't exciting?"

He chuckled. "You have no idea." Unable to stand it any longer, he brought his mouth to hers in a soft, tender kiss.

At first.

But the longer their tongues twirled around, tasting and savoring, the more passionate the kiss became. He was torn between wanting to get lost in her body and the desire to simply be in the same room. While taking her to bed was always in the back of his mind, that hadn't been why he wanted to see her tonight.

He'd missed her and that was the honest truth.

She slid her hand down to the center of his chest, pulling back. Her lashes fluttered over her intense blue eyes. "Mmmmm. That was nice."

"I'd say so." He ran his thumb over her lower lip. "Did you get your tire put back on?"

She dropped her head and moaned. "That's what you're thinking about right now?"

"That's what I'm using to stop myself from asking to see the inside of the master bedroom," he said. No point in lying anymore. "But also, I want to know if my buddy told you his thoughts."

"That's a buzzkill." She took him by the hand and tugged him toward the bar where she held up a bottle of wine.

"Do you have any beer?"

"There's some in the fridge. Help yourself."

"I'm sorry to have killed the mood. I hope to recreate it shortly." He strolled into the kitchen and pulled out a cold one. Leaning against the island, he cracked it open and gulped while staring at the most gorgeous woman he'd ever seen.

She poured herself a small glass and sipped. "I did take care of my tire. But your friend was nice enough to come to my office and deal with it because of my schedule. I didn't really get a chance to talk to him. Why?"

Scout rubbed his temple. "There was no slow leak. No hole. Someone had to have let the air out and that makes me nervous." Now he was really going to destroy any chance of things getting really heated tonight. "Have you had any run-ins with Kyle lately?"

She joined him in the kitchen, positioning herself between his legs. She continued to sip her wine, taking her time to answer.

He didn't like it.

"I can't tell you some things," she said.

"Patient confidentiality stuff?"

"Exactly," she said. "However, I believe I've finally made myself clear on the rest of it."

"I hope so. Unfortunately, that doesn't change the fact I think he sabotaged that tire."

"Why? What purpose would that serve?"

Scout chugged his beer. He twisted his body, setting the empty on the counter. He wrapped his arms around her waist. "I don't pretend to understand a guy like Kyle, but my guess would be to play hero."

"How does he do that?"

"He shows up when you realize it's flat and changes it. Or has it towed. And he can act like he saved the day."

"You mean like you did." Her entire body was pressed so hard against his they had become connected.

He liked the sensation.

"Not exactly what I did," he said, knowing she teased, but to him, this was serious business. "But he could have meant to scare. Or who knows what he was thinking, but I don't trust him based on what I saw and I kind of have a bit of an overprotective streak."

"I don't do that well." She cocked her head. "You have no reason to be jealous of Kyle."

"I didn't say I was." He tucked his hand under her shirt, massaging gently up and down her bare back. He found it interesting that she would even think he'd be jealous of Kyle. Not even remotely. "However, I was concerned for your safety while I was gone. That goes with being in Delta Force. Something that can't be changed in my personality, but I can do my best to be aware of it and not smother you."

"I appreciate that."

He fiddled with the small metal clasps of her bra. "But your tire didn't deflate itself and whatever might have happened that you can't discuss with me, please consider calling me if Kyle ever reaches out or shows up or does anything remotely inappropriate. Can you do that for me?"

"On one condition."

"What's that?" he asked.

"You get naked and follow me to my bedroom." She pushed off the center of his chest and lifted the shirt over her head.

"I might need a little more enticement."

"Oh. Okay." She reached behind her back. Her bra loosened off her skin. The straps slowly fell off her shoulders.

He groaned.

Her hands slipped under the fabric, cupping her breasts before she let the flimsy undergarment fall to her feet.

"You're covering up all the good stuff."

She shrugged. "I might be more motivated if you took off your shirt."

He tugged it over his head and tossed it to the kitchen table.

"Impressive, but I've already seen you shirtless."

"You're killing me." He undid the button on his jeans and lowered the zipper. He'd never been shy when it came to sex. But standing in the kitchen with this half-naked vixen, he was completely out of his element. He had idea what to do next, except he did know he'd do whatever she asked.

"You keep lowering those and I'll keep lowering these." Her right hand dipped just enough for him to see the darkening top of her nipple.

"How about I just drop them." He didn't wait for a response. He removed the rest of his clothing.

Her eyes grew wide and her hands lowered.

That was certainly the effect that he desired. He

inched closer. His chest heaved up and down with every labored breath. He never wanted anyone more than he wanted Talullah.

He pressed his lips against her neck while his hands worked on removing her pants. As he lowered her slacks, he lowered his kisses, making sure he gave each breast the kind of attention it deserved.

He was rewarded with a scalp massage and soft moans.

At this point he didn't care if he ever made it to her bedroom because he planned on devouring her right here, right now.

He lifted her off the floor.

"Whoa. What are you doing?" she asked.

"This." He set her on the counter. Spreading her legs, he lifted them over his shoulders and dived in, letting her hot juices coat his tongue. She tasted like sweet pineapple. Instantly, he became drunk and he selfishly wanted more. His desire to feel her body quiver against his tongue fueled his passion. He became relentless in his quest.

He reached up with one hand, pinching and twisting her hard nipple, enjoying how she arched and moaned with each lap of his tongue and tug at her breast.

Her hips roughly rolled against his mouth. Her

moans became louder and louder, bouncing off the walls, filling his ears.

"Yes. Yes," she said breathlessly. "Scout. Please. Yes." Her one heel dug into his back. She gripped his head, holding it to her for a long moment. Her muscles twitched and jerked as her climax filled his mouth. "Scout. I want you inside me."

Who was he to argue. He lifted her off the counter.

She pushed him to one of the kitchen table chairs and straddled him.

He swallowed hard as he watched himself disappear inside her. Gripping her hips, he held her steady. He needed a moment to catch his breath.

She cupped his face, kissing his lips with nothing but pure passion. Her hips rocked gently back and forth.

With that motion, he lost all control. As if he ever had it. Whatever she wanted, he would give to her. However she wanted it, he would make it happen. If this was what pleased her, it pleased him.

And make no mistake, he was fully satisfied.

All he could do now was hope to last long enough that she'd pull a second orgasm out of her body. He'd do whatever he could in his power to ensure that happened. He focused all his energy on her pleasure. Not his own.

She dug her nails into his shoulders and tightened herself around his length.

Her climax collided with his in an explosion of unbridled passion. His breath caught in his throat. He couldn't fill his lungs. His muscles shook from the inside out.

He'd had great sex before. But there were no words to describe what he just experienced.

She dropped her head to his shoulder and sighed.

"I would still like to see your bedroom," he managed between ragged breaths.

"That can be arranged," she said. "But right now, I'm oddly hungry."

"Me too," he said.

"I have leftover pizza in the fridge."

"That sounds amazing. Are we allowed to eat it in bed?" He lifted her chin with his thumb and forefinger. "Or am I being too presumptuous to think I might be allowed to spend the night."

Her smile brightened the entire room. "You are so adorable."

"Why?"

"Most guys would assume they were."

"I don't make those kinds of assumptions. Not

this early on." He kissed her plump lips. "But make no mistake. I like you. A lot."

"The feeling's mutual, but you should know, I have to get up early and go to work in the morning."

"No worries," he said. Since he'd been deployed on an assignment that they hadn't planned on, he was given a day off. But he knew he'd be up at the crack of dawn anyway. "I'll get up with you and be out of your hair."

"I didn't mean you'd have to leave."

He patted her naked bottom. "I know. But I haven't been home in almost four days. I have things I need to do, and then I was hoping we could do more of this tomorrow night."

"I think that can be arranged," she said. "How about you get the pizza and I'll go cozy up in bed."

"Sounds like a good plan." If Scout had any thoughts of putting the brakes on this relationship, they had long left the building.

CHAPTER 9

There was nothing worse than having a morning shower with the sexiest man alive interrupted before it began with a call from the hospital.

But that's exactly what happened.

Not only that, but Talullah had to put the brakes on getting frisky.

Worse, she couldn't give Scout all the details, but he was a smart man and he caught on real quick it had something to do with Kyle. She promised him she'd be safe and stay in touch, but other than Kyle going off the deep end where his daughter was concerned, there was no reason for Scout to be worried.

Not for her safety.

She strolled into the emergency room and found Brittany's chart.

"Hey, Talullah," Doctor George Baits, one of her partners, said. "Sorry to drag you in this morning."

"What happened, George?" She glanced down the hallway. A police officer stood by one of the curtains.

"Young Miss Brittany Diel has a broken wrist and a few bruises."

Talullah rubbed the back of her neck. George was a good doctor, but sometimes getting him to get to all the pertinent details was like pulling teeth. "And how did that happen?"

"Kyle brought her in around six this morning after her mom dropped her off at her dad's for a special birthday breakfast. Kyle said that he noticed Brittany rubbing her wrist and other bruises and when he asked his daughter, she told him Jim did it."

"And is that the story Brittany told the doctors?"

"She's slipped up twice saying she fell off her swing yesterday," George said. "Mom and Jim showed up about a half hour before you. We've managed to keep everyone separated. Mom and Jim are in the ER waiting room, and Dad is in the lounge, going ballistic I might add."

"All right. Let me go chat with Brittany. Alone. No social worker. No cop. Just me."

"Go for it."

Talullah took the chart, just in case she needed it for something. She smiled at the officer, showing her medical badge. He nodded.

She pulled back the screen.

"Doctor Rossi." Brittany adjusted herself on the gurney, setting aside her tablet. "They said you were coming."

Talullah rolled the chair over and sat down. "How's the wrist feeling?"

"It still hurts, but it's much better since they put a cast on it."

"I'm sure," Talullah said. "I've heard a couple of different stories about what might have happened."

Tears filled Brittany's eyes. "I didn't want to get anyone in trouble."

"I can understand that, but can you imagine how scary it must be to wonder if you're going to be punished for something you didn't do?" Talullah said, taking the girl's hand. "You've told two different stories. I need you to tell me the one that's real."

Brittany lowered her gaze and sniffled. "Jim did this to me. I didn't want to be a tattletale."

"I know this is all frightening. And you're being asked to be a grown-up and that's not fair. No one, especially your parents, should be putting you in this position. But I need you to be honest with me. I know you're worried about what might happen to you, but I can protect you from that."

She shook her head wildly.

"It's okay."

"You don't understand. That is the story I have to tell." For an eight-year-old, the girl enunciated every syllable clearly. But her wide eyes gave away all the fear that must have consumed her little body.

"Listen. I'm on your side. And if someone is hurting you, no matter who they are, I want to make sure they stop. But did you fall off the swing set?"

"But he's going to make my daddy go away. My mom and Jim didn't tell you that, did they," Brittany said in a huff.

"What do you mean make him go away?"

"My dad told me all about the custody thing and if he doesn't get some and my mom and Jim get it all when they get married, I won't ever be allowed to see him again."

Talullah tilted her head. "Your mom getting married has nothing to do with whether or not you can see your dad."

"My dad told me that once Jim marries my mom, he's my stepdad and he can get all the custody stuff with my mom and cut my dad out. The only way to make sure that doesn't happen is to make sure Jim doesn't marry my mom, or I might never see him again."

"Sweetheart, that's not how custody works." Talullah had half a mind to wring Kyle's neck. What a horrible way to use a child. But now she had another problem on her hands. She had no idea what Kyle would do to this poor kid when he found out she'd told on him, but the worst part of that statement was that Kyle didn't deserve custody, much less visitation at this point. "But I want you to understand something; what your father is doing is wrong."

"No, it's not. He's protecting me."

"How is lying a good way to protect you, especially when that lie is so harmful that it could potentially put an innocent man in jail? Do you understand that's what could happen to Jim if you press this lie with the police?"

She shook her head. "My dad said they would just question him and tell him he couldn't be around me anymore."

"If you continue with this story, because of the

last accusation that Jim hurt you, there will be an investigation. The police will come to your home and ask you all sorts of questions. It won't end here. It will uproot yours and your mother's life." Talullah squeezed Brittany's hand. "I'm being honest with you because I want you to truly comprehend what is happening. I care a great deal for your well-being and I don't want to see you go through this and I certainly don't want to see an innocent man go to jail."

"I don't either." She squeezed her eyes closed. Tears dribbled down her cheeks to her chin and onto her hospital gown. "But my dad. He's going to be disappointed. He'll be very angry with me."

"What do you think he will do?"

Brittany blinked. "Oh. I don't know. But sometimes he doesn't speak to me for days when he's upset over things that he says Mommy caused him to do. He can't control that, and then he needs space and he can't talk to me when he gets like that. It's all because of Jim. If he hadn't come into Mommy's life and brainwashed her, then things would be different. I'm only doing this to help my daddy."

"If I bring in a doctor friend of mine, and a special person from the police department whose only job is to protect you, will you repeat all this again?"

"I'm scared."

"I know. But I'll be right here. I promise you."

"What about my dad? He's going to be so mad."

"Would you feel better knowing he wasn't in the hospital anymore and that you might not have to see him for a bit?"

Brittany nodded.

"You hang tight. I'll be back soon." She stepped from the room and blew out a puff of air. She turned and faced the police officer. "No one but hospital staff gets in this room. Got it?"

"Yes, ma'am."

"Can you tell me who interviewed the father?"

"I did," the officer said. "The name's Officer Barnaby." He held out his hand." I also spoke with the mother and fiancé."

"And what were your thoughts?"

"The father's full of shit. He's hyperfocused on the fiancé and what struck me as most telling is that the dad constantly gave information that I didn't ask for."

"What about Jim?"

"Scared shitless, but all he cared about—and keeps asking about—is Brittany and is she okay. Are her needs being met. Has her pediatrician arrived. He comes off as a caring man who's more concerned about the kid than himself and it's genuine if you ask me."

"The social worker is on her way. Her name is Alice Gibbs. Please ask her to have me paged when she gets here if I'm not right in the area. I promised the little girl that I'd be here."

"I'll make sure we come and find you."

"Just make sure Kyle Diel doesn't come anywhere near her."

"That's why I'm standing here, ma'am."

"Thanks." She took the opportunity to head toward the main cafeteria for some decent coffee and maybe a breakfast sandwich. She stepped into the hallway and rounded the corner, skidding to a stop, wishing she had opted to stay in the emergency department.

"I was hoping to find you," Kyle said with more of a sneer. "I've been trying to reach you, but you're ignoring my texts and phone calls. I need your help right now. My daughter needs you and you can't be bothered?"

"That's not what's happening," she said behind gritted teeth. She glanced over her shoulder, but the automatic doors had swung closed, and the officer standing on the other side couldn't see her through the small window.

She was on her own.

Squaring her shoulders, she prepared herself for whatever crazy Kyle would bring.

"Are you kidding me? Have you even bothered to speak to Brittany yet?"

"I'm not going to speak to you while you're this upset."

"I have every right," Kyle said. "My precious little girl was beaten. I think that is cause to be pissed off."

Talullah had enough of playing this game. "If you think for one second I'm falling for this load of crap, you've got another thing comin'."

"Excuse me?" He took a step back and narrowed his stare. He gave her the once-over, planting his hands on his hips. He looked as though he just ate a lemon. "I'm not sure why are treating me this way. Or my child. I thought we had something special." He reached for her forearm.

The muscles in her body tensed. She jerked from his grasp. In all the years she'd known Kyle, she'd never been afraid of him. Ever. Of course, it had only been in the last year that he'd been more interested in Talullah outside of the office. But even then, he seemed harmless.

Only right now, she wasn't so sure.

His eyes were hard. Intense.

He had this nervous twitch as well.

But her area of expertise was in pediatric care. And specifically, general health. She knew nothing of the potential dangers that stared back at her. However, she knew enough not to be stupid.

"I'm sorry, Kyle. There is nothing for us to discuss right now."

"You're my daughter's doctor. I want to know what's going on with her. Take me to her right now." He inched closer.

She took two steps back. "Don't make me call security." She dug her hands into her white lab coat pockets and curled her fingers around her cell phone. "I suggest you take a different approach regarding this situation. Now if you will excuse me, I have some things to take care of." She turned on her heel and made a beeline for the emergency room doors. She placed her badge over the keypad and tapped her foot on the tile while glancing over her shoulder.

"What? Are you scared of me now?" Kyle called.

She ignored his heckling. Once on the other side of the door, she let out a long breath.

The officer noticed her as she leaned against the wall.

"Are you okay?" Officer Barnaby asked.

"Yes," she managed. "Please make sure that child's father doesn't get through that door."

"Did he harass you? Because I've gotten two separate reports he's making a menace of himself and security is ready to throw him out."

"That's not a bad idea," she said. "Though he didn't threaten me or anything and until we have the social worker's final notes to send to the judge, it might not be the right move."

"I hear you, but if he bothers you again, let me know."

"I will." For now, she needed to find a corner to catch her breath. That wasn't an easy thing to do in the ER, but she found an empty room and drew the curtain. She sat in the chair and pulled out her cell. "Hey Siri. Call Scout."

It rang three times before he picked up.

"Hi, Talullah. How goes things at the hospital?"

"Not wonderful," she admitted. Things had taken a huge turn and while she couldn't mention anything about Brittany, Talullah couldn't let go of the idea that Kyle could have deflated her tire. "Kyle's here."

"My overprotective instincts are trying to rear their ugly heads. But why?"

"Some of the details I can't get into. However, I'll allow you some leeway on this."

"What happened?"

"Do you really think he could have sabotaged my car the other night?"

"The only way for the air to come out of your tire was for there to be a leak. Or damage. Or for someone to have deflated it. The first two have been ruled out. You tell me."

She pinched the bridge of her nose. "What are your plans for the rest of the day?"

"I just got back from my run, and I was about to mow my lawn before taking a shower. Why?"

"Would you mind being by your phone?"

"I'm thinking I'd rather come to the hospital."

"I might not be more than an hour. Or this could go on for a while," she admitted.

"That's fine. I'll clean myself up and be there with a breakfast sandwich in forty-five. Sound good?"

"Are you sure you don't mind?"

"What are boyfriends for when they have a day off?" he asked. "Besides, I'm sure someday I'll need a return favor."

She laughed. "You've got yourself a deal."

CHAPTER 10

Scout stepped into the ER waiting room holding a hot coffee and an egg sandwich. Immediately his skin began to itch. He'd seen his fair share of hospitals, as a patient, but regardless, he'd be happy to see Talullah. He approached the nurse behind the desk. "I'm here to see Doctor Talullah Rossi. She's expecting me."

The nurse gave him the once-over. "Her typical patient is much younger."

A male in scrubs who stood a few feet away from the nurse chuckled. "And not half as sexy."

"Thank you. I think," Scout said.

"You must be Scout," the man said. "I'm her favorite nurse, Wayne. Follow me."

"Whatever you say."

The other nurse fanned herself. "If you're not her new boyfriend, I volunteer."

"I'll keep that in mind if she tosses me curbside."

"Sigh. Then it is true," the nurse said. "I don't know who's luckier. You, because that woman is a great catch. Or her, because just damn."

"I'm the lucky one."

"Oh. My uterus just weeped," the nurse said. "I'm dying over here and I want to take you with me."

"Just be quiet," Wayne said as he appeared at the doors that magically opened. "Ignore her. She's like this with all straight unavailable men."

"I don't think anyone has ever ogled me like that before."

"Oh. Stick around. After the night we had in this place, eye candy is precisely what we need."

"I feel so used."

Wayne laughed. "When Talullah said a friend of hers was coming, she didn't correct us when asked if he was male and her boyfriend. I understand why. But it's even better that you have a sense of humor. That girl needs a man who can make her laugh."

Scout paused in the middle of the hallway. "She's going to have my head for this, but what can you tell me about Kyle Diel?"

"If I wasn't gay and in a committed relationship,

I'd be asking to be your baby daddy," Wayne said. "Between you and me and these awful florescent lights, Kyle is an asshole."

"You know him well?"

"He's a pharmaceutical rep who calls on this pediatric ER as well as many local doctors' offices. That part is no big deal. But he got weird when his wife filed for divorce. He started recruiting people to be on *his side.* He tried to sprinkle bread crumbs that his ex-wife was a bad mother and all that. He's said and done some weird shit."

Scout didn't want to be on the bad side of Talullah, but he needed to understand some things while he waited for his buddies Lance and Liam, the two single men from his team, to finish digging on Kyle, which could take more than the forty-five minutes it took for Scout to make it to the hospital. "I don't know what Talullah has told you about my visit today, but I know Kyle is here."

Wayne arched a brow.

"I also know that she went out on a date with him a while ago—in hopes to get him to leave her alone—"

"For the record, I told her that was a mistake."

"I'm not going to argue that point, but, and this might be the craziest thing of all, is there any chance that all of this could be an insane attempt to get her to notice him? To acknowledge his existence and that she shouldn't have discounted him?"

"That's an interesting theory, but he'd be a sick and twisted bastard to use his daughter in the manner to which he has."

"I don't know about that detail."

"And I shouldn't have given it to you." Wayne held up his hand when Scout opened his mouth. "Talullah is a great pediatrician. The best. But we only see her around here when something happens to one of her kids that requires her to visit and that's not that often. Otherwise, she's upstairs when a baby is born. We don't see her interactions with Kyle. That happens mostly at her office. The only reason I know is I moonlight at her office, taking shifts when someone is on vacation." Wayne glanced around. He scratched the back of his head. "I was at the office a couple of times when Kyle showed up. He doesn't take no for an answer. He pushed Talullah into that date and trust me when I say it was a pity one. I wouldn't be surprised if all of this was to get her attention. But right now, the focus has to be a little girl who is—well, I can't say."

"I get it." Scout didn't need to be hit over the head with what could be going down. He certainly didn't want to jeopardize a young girl or any case that might be building one way or the other. Even though he had no idea what it was about, he had put together a pretty good idea in his head. Whatever it was, the fact he was standing in the ER, it wasn't good. "I'm here because Tulullah asked me to come with some breakfast." He waved the bag. "And she did mention a little bit about Kyle. I think something spooked her when it comes to Kyle. I only want to protect her and if in the process, I help her patient, that's a bonus for me."

"I like the way you think," Wayne said. He grabbed him by the arm and tugged him into the center of the emergency room. He pointed toward a cop. "That officer is standing watch over Kyle's daughter. In essence, making sure Kyle doesn't go and see his kid while the social worker and other doctors figure out the truth. If the system works, Kyle will be the one who is punished, but sadly, what he did won't send him to jail."

"You're not supposed to be telling me this."

Wayne shrugged. "I haven't told you anything medically."

Scout wasn't going to argue anything with Wayne. He was appreciative to have the intel.

"Besides. You're in the ER. There are lots of ways

for you to find out information." Wayne leaned against the counter and tapped a file. "You could be standing here waiting for Talullah and all sorts of things could fall into your lap."

"My God, man. You're pure evil. Or genius. Or both."

"I'll go with genius." Wayne winked. "If you ever decide you're gay and I decide to leave my husband, let's look each other up."

"Sounds like a good plan." Scout set the coffee and bag of food on the counter before he started glancing through Brittany Diel's chart. He only needed the basics, which jumped out at him.

Broken wrist.

Accused mother's fiancé.

Second story was she broke it on a swing set.

Social worker interview ordered.

Patient has admitted to lying about how injury happened and that father coached her on more than one occasion.

Fuck. That wasn't good.

"What are you doing?" Talullah's voice rang out so loud that Scout thought it came from inside his own head.

He swallowed his breath.

"Nothing."

"Don't lie to me," she said.

"Fine. I'm snooping."

She slammed the file shut, nearly taking his fingers off.

"Ouch." He shook out his hand for dramatic effect, though based on the scowl on her face, he didn't think it worked.

"You know better." She took the coffee and small bag from the counter. "Is this for me?"

"Yes," he said.

"Come with me."

"Yes, ma'am."

"God. I hate that," she said.

And he hated it when the women in his life were mad at him, but he had no one but himself to blame.

"What the hell do you think you were doing?" Talullah dragged Scout into one of the rooms that weren't being used. She kept her voice in a hushed tone just in case someone was listening, although everyone was busy taking care of their own cases and those that were around, and involved in hers, weren't in earshot.

Even so, she pulled the curtain closed.

"Waiting for you." He raised his hands. "And taking advantage of the opportunity that presented itself."

"At least you're honest."

"Unless I have to because of my job, I won't ever lie to you. Even if it sucks for me." He leaned against the gurney. "You called me here and not just because you wanted hot food and a decent cup of coffee."

"You're right about that," she said. "I just don't know how to ask for your help without putting my medical license in question."

"Well, now we're getting somewhere," he said. "This is new territory for me as well. But I think a good place to start would be to tell the police officer at your patient's door that I'm your bodyguard. Tell him what happened with the tire, so that there is a record of that, and—"

"I don't like mixing my personal and professional life."

"I know and I understand that. I don't either, but Kyle didn't leave you any other alternative. This isn't something you're choosing to do. And trust me. I want to spend time with you. But not like this. I don't mind sharing you with your colleagues or your patients. That goes with the territory as much as it does you sharing me with my teammates and the country, in a weird way, but Kyle is interjecting himself into our dating life. You have to—"

"Well, so is Crystal. She stopped by while you were gone." Shit. Talullah didn't want to go there. It wasn't fair and had nothing to do with the situation at hand. All it served was to change the subject and while that might ease the tension she felt in her bones, it didn't help the situation. If anything, it made it worse.

"She did what?" He cocked his head, shifted his stance, and folded his arms across his chest.

"Crystal came by my house to inform me about how you and your family work and how our helicopter ride was simply a ploy to make her jealous."

"And you believe that?"

"Not the point." She couldn't believe she'd even brought it up. Dumbest fight ever, but she wasn't about to back down now. She needed to commit if only to prove a point. Though she wasn't exactly sure what that point was at the moment, except for maybe that she didn't like to be controlled. Or maybe protected. Hell, she had no idea. She simply felt backed into a corner.

Trapped.

"Do you want to tell me what is? Because while I'm angry as shit about Crystal showing up, there isn't a damn thing I can do about it. And based on what happened between us last night and this morning, I believe it's safe to assume that her bullshit didn't affect you. I'm sorry that she invaded your space and said whatever. I'll address any of it with you when you're ready. But please don't use that to deflect whatever is going on with what Kyle is doing right now. Unless Crystal is threatening to harm me, you, or a child, we're talking about two entirely different types of people."

Talullah turned. She lifted the curtain and peered outside. Officer Barnaby still stood tall at Brittany's room.

Last Talullah heard, Doctor Alice Gibbs, the social worker, was still about twenty minutes out from interviewing Brittany.

And then she needed to talk with each of the parents and the authorities. It could be all day before anything was decided and that terrified Talullah.

"I'm sorry. That was out of line," she said. "Crystal has nothing to do with this."

"Maybe not, but she upset you."

Talullah turned and caught his gaze. "She did."

"I'm sorry she did that. What is it that you need from me?"

Even though this wasn't the time or place, since

Alice hadn't arrived yet, Talullah might as well take the time to discuss the uncomfortable parts of his past relationship so he could possibly have this one.

"Do you test the women you date when it comes to money and your heritage?" Shit. Nothing like putting all your cards on the table. "Before you answer, let me tell you why—"

"You don't need to add a why," he said behind a tight jaw. "I know why."

"Don't speak for me." She turned, facing him dead-on. "You asked what I needed and I asked a question. If you're going to get indignant, don't put yourself in the flame."

"Okay. I guess that's fair," he said. "But I still don't need the why because either Gillian told you or you figured it out on your own since you're a smart woman." He ran a hand across the top of his head. "Yes. I want to know how girls I date respond to money. I can't help it. It goes with the territory and it's always worse when someone knows who I am."

"I'm sorry that you believe most women are after you for your family money. I'm not."

"I never said you were and why are we having this fight? It has nothing to do with the problem at hand."

"It might not have anything to do with Kyle, but

it has everything to do with how I'm feeling about you right now." She paused to take a breath. "I just want to know why you feel the need to play games. What is it that you hope to find? Or are you just trying to trick—"

"Okay," Scout said, shaking his head. "I'm not really sure what we're going to accomplish by doing this right now, but since you asked the question, I'm going to answer it."

Talullah had to admit she was grateful for that, although she was still grappling with why she'd started the argument in the first place. Sure, she wanted to know why, but it wasn't a moral imperative and she hadn't felt as though it applied to her. Yet.

"I've dated two kinds of women in my life. Girls like Crystal, who see a lifestyle that they covet. They can say they have deep feelings for me all they want, but like with Crystal, the second they don't get all the jewelry, the cars, and the big house, they are out the door."

"Maybe. But she's still knocking."

"But I'm not answering." He laughed. "Thing is she found out my dad put money into a trust for me a long time ago and she wanted access." He held up his hand. "But that's type one. After money. The second type is the girl who thinks its sexy to be with someone in Delta Force. That's gross in a different way."

"Are you telling me that every woman you've ever been with has used you?"

"Maybe everyone except my high school sweetheart and you." He reached out and took her chin. "Please explain why we are having this ridiculous fight?"

"I wish I had one that made sense. But I don't." Gently, she curled her fingers around his wrist. "The way Kyle is behaving got me thinking about how ballsy it was of Crystal to show up at my house, unannounced."

"That's out there, even for Crystal," Scout said, rubbing the back of his neck. "I can see her approaching you at a bar, or even here at the hospital—"

"Wait. She works here?"

"She's done some moonlighting here. But she works at the rehab facility around the corner."

"She probably knows Kyle," Talullah said. "Gillian mentioned Crystal was babbling at the hair salon about how you were in your helicopter to make her jealous."

"Wonderful. That's all I need," he mumbled.

"If she's talking like that to a bunch of women in the beauty parlor, imagine the kind of attention she'd get from Kyle."

"Oh shit," Scout said. "Especially if they started dropping out names and putting it all together."

"And forming a plan." Talullah shook her head. "But why bring in an innocent little girl and make her lie?"

He tapped her temple. "Bigger picture." He tapped her temple. "Kyle filed for custody. This isn't only about you seeing him as the great stand-up man he wants you to believe he is, but to become father of the flipping year."

"Not on my watch," she said. "Now, I'm going to go tell that officer about the tire." She snagged the paper bag with the sandwich. "Are you going to follow me and guard my body?"

"I have to say, I'd rather be doing something else with it."

"I know a good broom closet around the corner." She kicked up her heel, glanced over her shoulder, and blew him a kiss.

Someone whistled.

Another person shouted something to the effect of, "You go, Doc Rossi."

And of course, Wayne had to make a comment

about the eye candy muscle on the sexy doctor's arm.

"I feel like half the room is undressing me," he whispered.

"It's more like everyone with a pulse." Talullah bit back a prideful smile. "They can look, but only I get to touch."

"That's the damn truth."

CHAPTER 11

Scout glanced at his cell. No new messages from either Lance or Liam. Or anyone else on the team for that matter. He leaned against the nurses' station and stared out across the room. A large group of people in scrubs scurried about the busy room.

"I don't know how you do it," he said to Wayne. "I couldn't do this job."

"And I can't stand around and look so damn pretty if I tried."

"I'm just a man." Hanging out with Wayne certainly would be good for Scout's ego.

"Who has muscles that everyone wants to touch? But they aren't over-the-top hard muscles. More like Goldilocks'."

"No one has ever compared me to a childhood

nursery rhyme. More surprisingly when the lead is a girl."

"No, dude. Just that you're f'ing perfect," Wayne said, waving his finger around in the direction of Scout. "You got the whole package and what's sad is, you don't get it."

"Standing in this room, I kind of understand why women get so upset when we men gawk at them."

"Yeah. That's never good. But we can do it when it's a beefcake like you. Sexism doesn't work in reverse."

"So I'm told," Scout said, stiffening his spine as the social worker drew back the curtain and stepped into the hallway, followed by another police officer. Talullah appeared about thirty seconds later. She gave him a slight smile and a nod. "What do you think happened?"

"Your guess is as good as mine. But here comes Talullah." Wayne lifted a chart from the desk. "Let me know the details."

"Will do." Not only was Scout invested in Talullah's world, but he found himself needing to know what happened to this young girl. "Hey." He reached out and squeezed her biceps. "Am I allowed to hug you here?"

"I think a warm embrace is called for after that."

She wrapped her arms around his middle and rested her head against his chest. "That poor girl is terrified."

"What happens now?"

"The social worker is calling the judge and asking that the mom be granted full temporary custody. She's asking that the fiancé not have any contact with the child during the investigation."

"Do they believe the boyfriend—"

"No. But there was an allegation. Just because it was recanted doesn't mean much right now. However, the child had some disturbing things to say about Kyle. If all goes as planned, he will be questioned, but this is where our system is flawed."

"So, they can't arrest him?"

"Technically, he hasn't done anything arrestable." She took a step back. "My partners have agreed to see all my patients at the office today, so I don't have to go in."

"That's nice of them."

"I don't want to leave until I know that little girl is with her mom and away from Kyle."

"I'm not going to leave this hospital without you." He arched a brow. "You can call me overprotective all you want."

"I'm not going to argue with you," she said,

letting out a long breath. She moved around him, pulling up one of the nurses' chairs and plopping herself in it.

Some commotion went on over by where the social worker stood.

"Is that the mom?" Scout wanted a visual on who the players were. He felt he needed that if he was going to be able to protect Talullah.

"Yes."

"Do you need to go over there?" He wanted to ask where the boyfriend was, but he figured he might have already left the building.

"No," Talullah said. "This is all in the hands of the social worker, the courts, and the judge. I might be called to testify. But unless that child needs medical attention, my role in this should be over."

"I don't trust that Kyle won't try to suck you in." Scout folded his arms and kept his gaze on that corner of the emergency room. "How do you feel about staying at my place this afternoon and tonight?"

"I don't want to be alone, so I'm not opposed to it. But I'm not going to live in fear forever."

"As you shouldn't. But until we know what his reaction's going to be, I'd feel better about things." Time to be totally honest. He turned, leaning over the counter. "I don't want you to be mad, but I'm having my buddies do some digging on Kyle."

She crossed her legs and swirled the chair back and forth. "That's the kind of stuff that makes me crazy. The police are here doing their jobs. They don't need you—"

"I reached out to my friends long before this morning happened. And I doubt the cops will care about the possible Crystal connection. Regardless, if we find anything that they need to know about, we'll pass it along."

"Just don't make a habit of doing stuff like that."

He laughed. "Are you forgetting who I am? Because being Delta Force kind of makes it a hazard of the job." He held up his hand. "But I promise not to be sketchy about it."

"I have no idea what that means." She pointed. "My patient and her mom are being escorted out. I think it's okay if we leave." She stood and ran her hand across his forearm. "I don't believe I've thanked you for being here for me."

"Anytime." He laced his fingers through hers and tugged. They weren't halfway across the emergency room when Kyle came flying through the doors after someone else opened them.

"Where is she? Where's Brittany? Where's my

kid? I demand to see her right now. You can't keep her from me."

"Shit," Talullah mumbled.

He pushed his arm out in front of her, tugging her in behind his frame. He scanned the area for the security guard or an officer, but found none.

Kyle must have been lurking in the shadows, waiting for his ex-wife and kid to leave, just so he could make a scene. Why though? What would be the point?

"I'm not the one who did anything wrong. I'm the one who brought her here. I'm the only one who is trying to protect her, and you people sent her home where she'll be subjected to a monster." Kyle stood near the door with his hands on his hips as a couple of people rushed toward him, Wayne being one of them.

"You need to leave," Wayne said.

"Not until I see my daughter."

Ha. Kyle had showed his ass since he'd already acknowledged that the staff had sent her home. Obviously, this was all showboating. Scout just needed to find the motivation. He had that, and he'd have a better picture into all the reasons why Kyle did anything.

Or so he told himself.

He'd read one too many of Jolene's books. His team leader Cannon's wife was quite the talent when it came to true crime fiction. She dropped you right in the thick of things. She wrote from the perspective of those around the crime and the details she included from those unique personal tales made each story richer.

It made the reader feel as though they were the investigative journalist, not Jolene.

"She's not here. Now, please don't make me call security. Or worse. The police. Because that won't look good for you," Wayne said.

Scout didn't believe appealing to Kyle's logic or even his emotions regarding the situation with his daughter would help de-escalate this situation. Crap.

Talullah.

That's what he wanted.

Her attention.

He wanted her to engage.

"Promise me no matter what you're not going to say a word to him," Scout whispered. "Not even if he gets in your face and directly confronts you in any way."

"Why wouldn't I respond?"

"Because you'd be feeding the beast and that's the

last thing we need. Let him leave here feeling defeated. As though he didn't accomplish his task."

"Won't that piss him off? Make it worse?"

"Do you trust me?"

"I let you defile my kitchen. Of course I trust you."

He chuckled. A sense of humor in this situation. Damn, he was in deep trouble with this woman.

His sister told him—and his mother agreed—when the right match came knocking, it would hit him like a ton of bricks.

Talullah came in like a high-speed train with no brakes.

But slow and steady always won the race.

No matter how strong his feelings grew for her, jumping into the deep end might not be a good idea.

"One more thing," he said. "Stay as close to me as possible. Unless I shove you away. And then find a desk to hide under because I don't want you to see me be a Neanderthal."

"You!" Kyle pointed at Scout. "What are you doing here? I bet you had something to do with all this bullshit, didn't you?"

Scout raised one hand. "I have no idea what you're talking about."

"Talullah. Why are you hiding behind him? Come

out and talk to me. Why are you doing this to me? To us? We had such a great thing going." Kyle lunged forward.

"You need to leave." Wayne stepped between Scout and Kyle. I'm not going to ask you again." He held up his cell. "Don't make me press that button."

Kyle took a step back. "This isn't over," he said. "Talullah. May I speak with you, please."

"You may not." Scout reached behind his back and squeezed Talullah's arm.

"I don't think she appreciates you answering for her." Kyle took a step to the right. "Talullah. This will only take a minute. We need to talk."

"No. You don't. Now leave or I will escort you out myself," Scout said.

"Are you threatening me?" Kyle glanced around, waving his hand like a wild bull. "Did everyone hear this man?"

"If you don't leave now, I'm calling the police," Wayne said. "There's the door. Use it."

"Talullah. I'll be in the parking lot. I'll wait ten minutes for you." Kyle turned on his heel and marched out of the emergency room. Once the doors shut tight, there was a collective sigh of relief.

Only, Scout didn't share in their enthusiasm.

This might be over for them, but it wasn't over for him and Talullah. This he knew for sure.

He turned, gripping her biceps. He stared into her blue eyes. "I don't trust that he won't either sit by your car and wait, or worse, be lurking in the shadows and follow you home."

She visibly shivered. "I don't want to leave my car here."

"Would you be okay if one of my friends comes and brings it home for you?" Scout asked.

"I would."

"Good."

"Thank you for asking and not taking over and just doing it." She raised up on tiptoe and kissed his cheek.

He groaned. "For the record, if you had put up a stink, I would have solicited Wayne and everyone else in this room to talk some sense into you. Or perhaps I would have just tossed you over my shoulder and carried you out to my car."

"If you ever do that to me in public, I might have to hurt you."

"Is that a promise?" He winked. He looped his arm around her shoulders. "Come on. Let's get you back to my place so I can pamper you for the day."

"Does that include a massage and foot rub?"

"That can be arranged along with a nice steak dinner, and then perhaps we can defile my kitchen."

"Sounds like a good plan."

To say he was in over his head was an understatement.

* * *

Talullah eased into the bathtub and closed her eyes. The hot water and bubbles coated her skin like silk. The stench of the day disappeared.

"Can I come in? I have wine and a snack," Scout said.

"Oh, my God. Please." She blinked, shifting in the massive standing tub that would easily fit two people. A pang of jealousy filled her soul like foul chicken. She swallowed, hoping to get rid of it, but it settled right in her gut.

The idea he shared this with the likes of Crystal made her want to vomit.

"You look like you just ate a lemon," he said as he placed a small bowl of freshly cut strawberries on the bathtub tray that his sister told him he had to have in case this very situation ever happened. He stood at the sink and wrestled with a bottle of wine, pouring it into two plastic stemmed glasses. He handed her one and stood awkwardly by the side of the tub. "Care to tell me what's wrong?"

"Not really. I'd rather you joined me."

He set his beverage next to the fruit and jumped from his clothes as if he were on fire. He sloshed into the bath like a little kid.

She laughed.

"I thought you were never going to ask."

"Trust me, I thought about being selfish and keeping this all to myself, but you brought sustenance." She lifted her glass and tapped it against his. "You deserve a little soak after that."

"This is nice." He leaned back and smiled. "Were you able to nap?"

She appreciated how easily he accepted it when she didn't want to speak about something. That took a certain amount of confidence to be able to do that and so far, she hadn't found anything that Scout appeared to be insecure over, except maybe the fact he believed almost all women were after his money.

She tried not to scowl.

"There's that look again," he said.

Obviously, she'd been unsuccessful. Her sister told her that she had no poker face at all.

In general, her sister was almost always right.

"I'm a horrible human being for even bringing this up while we're sitting naked in your bathtub."

"No. You're not." He leaned over and palmed her cheek. "You can talk to me about anything. I promise that if it upsets me, I'll try to keep that in check."

"I've never met anyone quite like you."

"I hope that's a good thing."

"So far, it's great." She took a dainty sip of her wine before setting it on the tray. "So, I went from being jealous of the fact that you lived here with another woman to wondering how you missed Crystal was after your money if you play all those stupid games."

He tapped the center of his chest with his fore-finger. "Ouch."

"Sorry. You asked and I'm being honest."

"I always knew Crystal enjoyed the finer things in life and when we first met, she knew who I was. She never pretended she didn't and I appreciated that about her, but what she did fake was her desire to have things right now. Or the fact that she wanted to quit working and live off my family's money. However, she posed that as she wanted to stay home and raise children, thinking that's what I would have wanted."

"You don't?"

He shrugged. "If I ever get married and have kids, that's a discussion to be had and whatever makes the most sense will happen. But there's nothing wrong with a mom having a career."

Damn, her uterus just sang.

"So when she moved in and started talking about ripping out walls and redecorating, I got a little nervous. I mean, this place needed a new kitchen and this bathroom needed to be redone, but that was all I could get on board with."

Talullah did her best to ignore the sudden heartburn. "So, she designed this? Picked out everything?"

"Anyone ever tell you that you're cute when you're jealous?"

"No," she said firmly.

He chuckled. "She had nothing to do with it. As a matter of fact, this was all only recently finished. My mom and sister did and on a budget I could afford on my salary. Not what Crystal wanted, so rest assured, there has never been any bathtub sharing with any other women. Just you."

"You are so about to get laid." She took a strawberry and placed it on her tongue.

He groaned.

"But first, I have to ask. If you knew she wanted your money, why did—"

"I also believed she loved me in spite of the wealth. I thought she was okay with us living within our means, only using that for the big things. Like a bigger house if we got married and had kids. One with a fancy backyard where I could build a massive swing set and have a pool. Not on expensive jewelry pieces, a hundred or so designer handbags, and a new car every year."

"Oh. I need the handbags. That's a moral imperative."

"Are we negotiating?"

"God, no." She tossed her head back and laughed. "In my budget, I have a line item for designer purses. I don't get mani-pedi's except for special occasions and I don't color my hair or anything like that. I like jewelry, but I buy costume pieces. But when it comes to shoes and handbags, I'm a whore."

He took her glass from her hand.

"What are you doing?"

"Setting our drinks and snack to the side." He pulled her between his legs. "I want to state for the record that I would never use that word to describe you."

"If you saw my purse collection, you might."

"Never." He took her mouth in a hot, passionate

kiss. His tongue swirled around hers, demanding attention and she responded in earnest.

She'd never been shy when it came to sex, but she wouldn't ever describe herself as a vixen. She enjoyed sex. A lot. But she had boundaries. Limits.

However, she saw herself pushing them where Scout was concerned. Not that she would do anything too out there, but she was feeling empowered in ways she had never felt before.

Sexuality came in degrees. Being comfortable in her own skin and feeling sexy was one thing. She owned that. It was something she believed every woman, no matter shape or size, had the ability to achieve. It didn't come from a man. His words and actions were fleeting. They might inflate those emotions; however, they didn't create them. Unfortunately, a man, or another woman, could destroy them in a flash.

She'd allowed that to happen once before. She would never do that again. She'd forever demand to be valued and appreciated for who she was both inside and out.

Scout treated her like an equal. He flexed his muscles today, only that was his area of expertise. Besides, she'd asked him to behave that way. And he certainly didn't act like a Neanderthal. He was the kind of man who—when necessary—would always take control of the situation. He'd defend who and what he cared for no matter what.

She could get on board with a relationship with a man like Scout.

His hands smoothed over her body as if she were clay and he was molding her into a piece of art. Every tender touch sent her closer to the edge. He pulled the plug and the water slowly began to drain.

Effortlessly, he lifted her out of the tub and set her on the bath mat. He took the terrycloth towel and dried her body. With every swipe of the soft fabric, he brushed his fingers across her skin as well. He pressed her against the vanity, raising her leg over his shoulder.

Threading her fingers through his hair, she watched as his tongue lapped across her hard nub. Her nipples hardened and tingled. Her breathing labored.

He arched up with one hand and cupped her breast, fanning his thumb.

She moaned, rolling her hips. Her orgasm started at her toes, curling them as it crawled up her calves before shooting across her body, making every muscle quiver in delight.

He kissed his way to her mouth. She'd never

wanted to taste herself on anyone before, but with Scout, it was the most natural thing she could possibly desire. She shifted her body, angling it enough to feel his hardness against her, and she drew him inside.

Then she pushed him away.

"What are you doing?"

Smiling, she lowered herself, all while making sure she kept eye contact. She took him into her hands and licked the tip.

He let out an audible groan and leaned back, gripping the countertop.

She continued on her quest, enjoying not only how she tasted, but him. This had never been her favorite thing to do. She'd always done it because she wanted to. There was a certain amount of sexual gratification to it, but she could also take it or leave it.

Not with Scout.

She wanted this.

Needed it.

It came with a sense of empowerment that she'd never experienced before.

A kind of control that she didn't know existed.

Power.

And she loved it.

"That's enough," he said with a throaty voice as he tugged at her hair. "Let's take this to the bed." He took her by the hand and led her to the master bedroom where he gently pushed her down on her back. "You're so beautiful."

Her breath hitched.

He stared at her so intently she couldn't form a coherent thought. He settled between her legs, entering her slowly.

Clinging to his shoulders, she raised her hips, selfishly wanting all of him right now, but he wouldn't allow it. He teased her with a small piece of him. Leisurely, he eased in and out of her while she tried to buck like a wild animal.

Only there was no curbing her appetite. Her body demanded more and she needed it now.

She wrapped her legs around his body, clasping her ankles together, and she squeezed as hard as she could, holding Scout in place while she grinded against him.

He groaned. He rolled her to her back and then separated their bodies.

"I'm not happy right now," she managed, staring at him from up on her elbows.

"Get on all fours and maybe I can make you ecstatic."

If a woman's uterus could weep, hers just did.

He grabbed her hips and pulled her back onto him.

She glanced over her shoulder and groaned as he entered her in a power thrust.

This time he did not go slow. There was no teasing. No mercy. He reached around and found her hard nub and fanned it gently with his finger, driving her mad with passion.

Her orgasm hit hard. She dropped her head and held the sheets, calling out Scout's name as his climax mixed with hers in a moment that would forever be engrained in her core memory.

It took a few minutes before she could catch her breath.

He collapsed next to her, pulling the covers over their bodies and adjusting the pillows. He held her body close to his, running his hand protectively, lovingly, up and down her arm.

Snuggling in closer, she closed her eyes. "I have to go into the office tomorrow," she whispered.

"I'm a little concerned about the possibility that Kyle might show up there."

"I can't say that thought hasn't crossed my mind, but my partners have agreed that he's not to be let in and George, the senior partner, will call the company Kyle works for and explain that we have to have a different rep and why."

"That does make me feel a little better, but that doesn't mean Kyle won't randomly waltz into the office and cause a scene. Or sit in the parking lot. Or follow you—"

"Okay. Can you stop freaking me out?" She blinked, glancing up at him. "Does your mind always go that dark?"

"My team leader's wife is a crime novelist and I'm her biggest fan. Sorry. I also can't help it. I think the guy's a creeper."

"I'm not going to argue with you on that point. But I don't need to be paranoid to and from work."

"I have to go to the base tomorrow, but maybe I can drive you back and forth? Please?" He kissed her forehead.

"I will let you do that." She pressed her hand on the center of his chest. "But only because of this Kyle situation. Once that is cleared up and I'm not wigged out or a little frightened, I drive myself and don't constantly spend the night."

"Okay, but we can spend them sometimes, right?"

"We can do weekends. Friday and Saturday nights. When I'm not on call."

"And one night during the week. Just one," he

said, holding up two fingers. "And two if we know I'm being deployed."

"We'll start with weekends for a month, and then we can add more."

"But you know you're going to want more sex than that," he said with an arched brow.

"We don't have to have sleepovers to do that."

He rolled his eyes. "You're killing me."

"That's the way it's going to be if you want to date me."

"Well, I'll warn you then, I tend to fall fast asleep after sex and I can't be woken up for at least four to seven hours. So, on that note. I'll see you in the morning." He gave her a quick kiss and settled in, closing his eyes.

She opted not to say another word. Instead, she hugged him tighter. Scout was the kind of man she could fall in love with.

Maybe she already was.

CHAPTER 12

Talullah set her last chart in the basket on the counter at the reception station. The day had ticked by slowly. Nothing bad had happened. There had been no Kyle sightings, which was good, and his company absolutely agreed to pull him from the account.

A full investigation was being conducted into all allegations, including the idea that Kyle had fully intended to make sure Jim either spent time in prison, or ended his time.

Talullah shivered.

According to Brittany, her father had kept telling her that Jim did these things to her and that he had to pay for them. That if she didn't do her part and tell the authorities what a bad man Jim was, then Kyle was going to have to take matters into his own hands. Kyle then told his kid that she would be responsible for whatever happened next.

That poor girl believed that Jim had been the reason her parents divorced and why her father couldn't see her as often as he liked. He had even told her that the times he'd canceled on his visitation were lies. He hadn't canceled at all. Jim had talked her mom into changing plans and there was nothing that Kyle could do. He was at their mercy and this was the only way Brittany would be able to see her dad.

However, the police had very little to go on. Just the words of a scared little girl who had changed her story.

That didn't help the situation.

"Hey, Talullah," Teresa said as she sat up and peered out the window. "The police are here."

"Seriously?"

Teresa nodded. "One cop car with a uniformed police officer and one dark sedan with two suits, and all three are headed this way."

Talullah sucked in a deep breath, preparing herself for anything.

The door opened and in strolled the two men wearing sports coats and slacks, followed by the police officer.

"Can I help you?" Talullah asked.

"We're looking for Doctor Talullah Rossi," one of the men said. "I'm Detective Marco Dorin. This is my partner Detective Eddy Quinn."

"I'm Talullah," she said. "Did something happen?"

Teresa rushed to her side and held her arm.

"Is there a place we can talk where there are no patients?" Marco asked.

"They've all left for the day. You can speak freely here, which I wish you would do because you're scaring me," Talullah said.

"We're sorry to do that," Eddy said. "This has to do with Kyle Diel."

"Maybe we should go to my office." She took Teresa by the hand and squeezed. "If Scout shows up, tell him what's going on and that I'll be out shortly."

"Who's Scout, ma'am?" Marco asked.

"My boyfriend," she said, ignoring the raised brow by Teresa.

"Is his last name Finch?" Eddy asked.

"Yes. Why?" Talullah's heart dropped to her gut.

The two detectives exchanged a glance between each other.

"He should be part of this conversation," Eddy said. "Are you expecting him soon?"

"I think he just pulled in." Teresa pointed toward the window.

"Perfect timing," Marco said.

Talullah wished her pulse would stop pounding in her throat, making it hard to swallow. She also found it difficult to hear anything other than her heart beating like a wild beast.

A few minutes passed in awkward silence.

The creaking of the door opening startled her. She wanted to run to the threshold and throw her arms around Scout. But instead, she stood stoic by the back hallway and smiled.

"Talullah? Is everything okay?" Scout closed the door and glanced around the room before making his move, weaving around the detectives so he could place his arm around her waist.

"These detectives are here to talk to us about Kyle," she said.

"What about him?" Scout asked.

"Is it okay if we sit down?" Marco waved to the chairs in the waiting room.

"Please." Talullah nodded. She laced her fingers

through Scout's and sat down across from the team of detectives.

Teresa went behind the desk and went to work filing the last of the charts from the day.

Scout lifted his arm and rested it on the back of her chair. "Did Kyle do something that we should be concerned about?"

"Yes," Marco said.

"What did he do?" Talullah squeezed Scout's knee. "He didn't hurt Brittany, did he?"

"No. However, during this investigation, we were able to get a search warrant for Kyle's house as well as his computer. During the search and seizure, we found enough evidence to arrest him on conspiracy charges. One of the conspiracies is to commit the murder of Scout."

Talullah gasped.

"Sweetheart, it's okay. I'm still breathing." He lifted her hand and kissed the back of it.

"Please don't make jokes. This is not amusing. The things that man has done to manipulate a child make me sick to my stomach." She glared.

"I'm sorry. I didn't mean to make light of the situation." Scout turned his attention to the detectives. "Did he make any other threats?"

"If you're asking if he threatened Talullah, the

answer is no," Eddy said. "However, he has an unhealthy obsession for her."

"What is that supposed to mean?" Talullah asked.

"We found images that paint a narrative where he sees you becoming his wife and the mother to his daughter. He's gone as far as cutting out his ex-wife from pictures and putting your face in her place," Marco said.

"That's seriously twisted," Scout said.

Talullah's stomach soured. "I knew he had a thing for me, but I had no idea it went that far."

"He believes you're his soulmate and that Scout is a minor complication that will soon be removed," Eddy said.

"Have you arrested Kyle?" Scout asked.

"That's the reason we're here," Eddy said. "We've been unable to locate him. When we executed the search warrant, he got pissed and left. He said he was going to work. He never showed at his office today. We have an all-points bulletin out for him, and we will find him, but considering the threat Kyle made, we needed for you to know. Unfortunately, we don't have the kind of resources to put someone at your front door, but we can increase patrols in your neighborhood."

"I appreciate that," Scout said. "Just so you're aware, I'm with the Army."

"I was going to ask what branch of the military you were with," Eddy said. "Please don't take this the wrong way, but we don't need any heroics. If you see Kyle or hear from him, call us. Don't take matters into your own hands."

"I won't entirely make that promise," Scout said. "I'm with Delta Force. I'm not saying that to brag, just to make clear that I have a certain skill set that if I'm threatened, or Talullah is, and waiting for you isn't an option, I will do what's necessary."

"Just don't give us a reason to have to arrest you." Eddy stood. "You will see an increased police presence both here and around your home."

"Once we have Kyle in our custody, we will let you know." Marco eased toward the door.

"I have one more question." Scout jumped to his feet and strolled across the room. "There is one person that you haven't mentioned that I'm personally concerned about."

"Who's that?" Marco asked.

"My ex-girlfriend." Scout glanced over his shoulder.

Talullah shouldn't be jealous. There was no reason to be, but she didn't understand why he'd be concerned with her at all. She had nothing to do with this.

"Who is she and why are you worried about her?"

"Her name's Crystal Manning. I'm not sure she's involved at all. However, she recently showed up randomly at Talullah's making strange declarations when I was deployed on a mission last week. She's a nurse and it's possible that she knows Kyle. Between her wanting to get back together with me, and Kyle being insanely delusional, I can't help but wonder if he put her up to that strange visit."

"Her name didn't come up anywhere on his computer or in our search of his home," Eddy said. "Do you think she could be hiding him?"

"I don't know," Scout said. "Here's her address." He held up his cell. "I don't believe she'd do anything that would put me, or anyone else, in danger. Not willingly."

"But you think she could be manipulated?" Marco asked.

"Kyle can be charming." Talullah felt the need to interject. She didn't want to defend Crystal or her actions. The way she'd treated Talullah had been unacceptable, but if Kyle was behind it, she'd bet her last dollar that he made sure Crystal believed confronting Talullah was the best way to get what she wanted.

Which was Scout.

Talullah wasn't quite sure how that played into making sure Scout was out of the way, but it didn't matter. What did was that everyone was safe, and that included Crystal.

"When he was first separated from his wife, he seemed like he was devastated. I would listen to him whenever he came into the office and as time went on, I got sucked into his humor. He can be funny," Talullah said.

"You're not at fault here, ma'am," Eddy said.

"I know that." She wanted them to understand that Crystal, if she was involved in helping him, might not be aware of anything Kyle has done. Or even if she knows, Kyle would find a way to make it everyone else's fault. "Kyle is a master at shifting the focus. Even I fell victim to it for a while. It wasn't until he started using those subtle manipulations to get me to go out on a date with him that I realized what he'd been doing. Crystal may not be aware of any of this."

"Was there anything in your investigation and search that indicates Kyle is armed and dangerous?" Scout asked.

"Yes," Marco said. "We're taking this very seriously."

Talullah grabbed Scout's biceps. "What about Elaine and Brittany? I worry that Kyle might take the bulk of his anger out on them at this point."

"We appreciate your concern," Marco said. "We are doing everything we can to protect them."

"Listen. My team has to be at the base tomorrow, but we are happy to lend our services over the weekend and possibly after that if Kyle still hasn't been found," Scout said. "I know I for one want to be of service."

"We'll be in touch." Marco stretched out his arm. "Thank you for your service."

"Yours as well," Scout said.

Talullah let out a long breath as she watched the two detectives leave her office. The uniformed police officer, who hadn't said a word, followed them. She leaned against Scout's strong frame. "I'm sorry I dragged you into this mess."

"You didn't drag me into anything." He wrapped his arms around her, tugging her close. "I think we should stay at my house tonight."

"I'm not going to argue with you about that, even though I think my bed is more comfortable."

He pressed his warm lips on her temple. "Any bed that you're in works for me."

"He's a keeper," Teresa said from the other side of the counter.

Talullah had to agree, but she wasn't ready to say that out loud. They needed more time to get to know each other better and settle into their relationship.

Relationship.

She'd wanted to be a part of a partnership for so long, but all the men she'd dated had fallen short of her expectations. At one point she thought perhaps she'd set her sights way too high, but the older she got, the more she realized she'd be settling if she went for anything less.

Scout checked all the boxes and then some.

However, she needed more time with him to be sure. No matter how much her heart fluttered when she was in his presence, she needed to be sure, and the only way to do that was to take the time.

And she'd have a lot of fun doing it.

"Oh. I don't know about that." Talullah patted his chest and glanced up, smiling. "But for now, I'll enjoy his company."

Scout didn't like the fact that Crystal hadn't returned his text or answered his call.

"Staring at your cell isn't going to make her respond any quicker." Talullah placed a plate of food in front of him.

He inhaled sharply. "That smells delicious."

"I'm not the best cook in the world, but I can do mac and cheese." She laughed.

"From scratch no less. That's a real talent."

"If you say so." She sat in the stool next to him at the island. His kitchen was half the size of hers, but it did the trick. And, since the remodel, it had all the latest, greatest features. Sure, it was missing some things that her kitchen had, like the double oven and subzero fridge, but he wasn't about to complain. He had more than what he needed.

For now.

He scooped a large forkful of food into his mouth. "Oh, my God. This is almost as good as you."

She slapped his shoulder. "You're a pig."

"No. I just have sex on the brain."

"That too."

He continued to nibble on his dinner, while trying not to glance at his cell every five seconds. He didn't want Talullah to think he carried a torch for his ex because he didn't. However, he was concerned for her safety.

Talullah touched his forearm. "We have to go on the concept that no news is good news."

"I wish I could," he said. "But considering how I know her, she'd be all over a text or call from me. And I don't say that to be conceited."

"I know."

He pushed his plate aside and lifted his beer, taking a hearty swig. "I only want her to be safe."

"Scout, you don't have to justify your concern for her well-being to me. I get it. I don't want anything bad to happen to Crystal either. I just hope she's totally unaware of how he's been manipulating and hurting his kid."

"Thank you for that."

Talullah palmed his cheek. "While I'd be lying if I didn't feel a slight pang of jealousy, it's only because you care deeply about people and I want to be someone that fits like that in your life."

He shifted, pulling her between his legs. "I care a lot about you," he said. "More than I can put into words right now and truthfully, I want to fight it."

"I know what you mean."

He smoothed his hands over her hips. "Had this

situation not escalated the way it did, we'd be able to slow all this down."

"I'm not sure I agree with that statement." She wrapped her arms around his shoulders and leaned into his frame. "It's possible that we could, but I don't believe we would." She kissed him tenderly. Her lips were soft and she tasted like sunshine on a warm summer's day. "I'd be telling myself that we're going too fast. That I shouldn't spend the night or that I should tell you to go home, but in the end, I'd cave."

"What about our agreement that sleepovers only happen on weekends?"

"That's still going to be a rule for a while."

"Why?" He tilted his head.

"Because I need my sleep." She arched a brow. "And I don't want to feel like we're living together in the beginning."

"That's a good plan," he said. "I can see us going the distance."

"Oh yeah? And what does that look like?" She sat back on her stool. The corner of her mouth twisted upward in a daring smile.

"This is where I'm going to get myself in trouble and scare you off," he said.

"I'm surprised I haven't already sent you packing.

I mean, we've been dating for a week and we're talking about a future."

He chuckled. "That is crazy." But he saw one with Talullah. It was as clear as day. The details might be fuzzy, but he could no longer picture his life without Talullah in it.

Crystal never had that kind of effect on him. No woman had.

"I'm waiting," Talullah said.

His stomach filled with butterflies. Not the adrenaline kind, but the ones a teenage boy got right before he kissed a girl for the first time under the bleachers. It wasn't fear. Nor was it excitement. It was the anticipation of knowing what you wanted but being unsure it would go as expected.

"There's this house in the Lampass River neighborhood."

"The one right on the river with the big pool house?"

"That's the one," he said.

"That place is gorgeous, but I bet if it ever went on the market, it would be ridiculously expensive."

"It would be pricey," Scout admitted. "The owner has listed once in the past year and I know he's going to do it again. It's just a matter of time. Anyway. I always said if or when I got married and had kids, I'd buy a house like that."

"Don't you think that's a bit over the top?"

"Not compared to how my parents are going to spoil my children." He snagged his beer and gulped. "Before my sister lost her baby, my parents bought every single thing Hannah and her husband would need. I mean everything."

"That must have been hard for them to have all that stuff after the death of their child." Talullah rested her hand gently over his. "I can't imagine."

"It's been really hard, but they are trying again. I don't ask because I figure they aren't going to tell me until they get past the three-month mark, which I understand."

"What about all the stuff your parents bought? Will they use that if they get pregnant again?"

"No. They donated it all to a shelter for battered women and children."

Talullah gasped, covering her mouth. "That is the sweetest thing I've ever heard."

"They didn't want to be reminded of what they lost and my parents thought it best that if they were blessed to have another baby they should have all new things."

"I think that makes sense, but I'm not sure how

I'd feel about someone buying all my stuff. I'd want to pick it out."

"Oh. My sister had final say on everything. My parents aren't that bad. But they won't let you pay for it. They constantly tell me that they can't take their money with them, so they want to spend some of it on us. And they do and I won't deny them the pleasure of buying for their grandkids. If we have them."

"You said we. How do you even know I want them?"

"Do you?"

She laughed. "I can see myself having a couple. But for a guy who worries about women being after them for his money, you're letting me in pretty deep."

"I am." He nodded. "I'm telling you right now, you have to get that designer handbag thing under control. That will put me in the poorhouse."

"That's funny. But I make my own money," she said. "Speaking of which, how does all that work if you buy a house like that. I mean, I can't afford it."

"I can't either on my salary. But it's one of those things I'd use my trust fund on," he said. "Anything for my family I can use that. So, a house. Or say a nice minivan for you."

"Oh no. I won't be driving one of those. An SUV is the only way I'm going to go."

"Point taken," he said. "And then there are expenses like sports and college funds or whatever else having children entails, but I don't want them to think just because they are a Finch that means that money grows on trees."

"You've given this a lot of thought."

"Not really. But ever since you walked into my life, I've thought about it more."

"Looks like we're going to explore this relationship in depth." She raised her finger and gave it a little waggle. "But when it comes to buying houses and cars and spending money, I don't want to ever be extravagant. I don't need those things. Well, I need the handbags."

"You're on your own with those." He leaned in to kiss her, but before his lips reached hers, his cell buzzed. He glanced at the screen.

Crystal.

Finally.

He tapped the answer button. "Hello? Crystal? Are you okay?"

"No. Actually, I'm not," Crystal said.

"What's going on?" Scout jumped from the stool. His heart lunged to his throat. "Are you with Kyle?"

"No," she said softly. "I haven't seen him since this morning. Can you come over? I'm scared he's going to come back."

"Come back?"

"He was here this morning talking about how his ex-wife had made up a bunch of lies about him and now she had Talullah on her side and was going to take Brittany, their daughter, away from him. He was so heartbroken over her and how she'd been manipulated by Elaine, Jim, and you."

"Me? I don't know any of these people."

"He told me you knew Jim from the base. He's a civilian, but works as a career counselor for military personnel making the transition to civilian life."

"I don't know him." Scout pinched the bridge of his nose. "Where is Kyle now?"

"I don't know. But he was acting weird and he texted me a little a while ago. He wants money and to borrow my car."

"What did you tell him?"

"I haven't responded. I'm supposed to still be at work, but they let me leave early. Can you please just come over? I'm scared."

"The police have increased their presence in your neighborhood," Scout said. "I'm going to text you a phone number for a detective. I want you to call him and tell him everything you've told me."

"Okay. I can do that, but will you still come over? I'll feel better if you're here."

Talullah shoved a piece of paper in front of him.

Have her come here.

He nodded. "Crystal. Get in your car and come to my place."

"I have my mother here. I can't. Please. I'm begging."

Scout rubbed the back of his neck as he paced in his small kitchen. Her mom was wheelchair-bound and had memory issues. Crystal and her siblings had put her in a nursing home a little over a year ago. It was rare that Crystal brought her back to her place anymore. It was too difficult because her mom needed so much care at this point.

"My mom is asking for you," Crystal said. "And she wants you to bring your new friend."

He stopped dead in his tracks.

Her mother was nonverbal.

That was a message.

Kyle had to be there and he wanted Scout, and Crystal just tipped him off.

"Well, if your mom wants me there, then who am I to deny her. I'll be over soon. I'll bring the salsa."

"Thanks. I appreciate it."

He tapped the screen, ending the call. "Fuck," he muttered. "Kyle is holding her hostage."

"How do you know?"

"Her mom can't speak and salsa is what she called my teammates and she always hated it when I had all of them over."

CHAPTER 13

"I'm not going to argue with you." Scout slammed the gear shift of his Jeep into park. "I told you earlier that I wouldn't promise that I would stay out of this if someone was in danger. I've given you all that I know and I get your hands are tied. Mine are not."

"Yes, they are," Marco said. "You're not a cop. I don't give a shit that you are Delta Force. In my eyes, and the eyes of the law, you're a civilian and you're going to be in the way."

"Listen. Me and my team will be in and out before you get all your ducks in a row," Scout said. "I didn't have to give you the courtesy of this phone call or all the details of our plan. You have the timing, to which if I don't hang up, will be off. So, if you show up before we've fully executed our mission, don't do anything to endanger my men or you'll have to deal with the full weight of the United States Army and I don't think you want to do that."

"Just don't get anyone killed, got it?"

"Got it." Scout tapped the cell. His heart hammered in his chest like it never had before. He'd been on many missions where he wondered if he was going to come back home in a body bag or not.

But none of those had him this hyped up.

He reached across his Jeep and opened his glove box, pulling out his personal weapon.

"You're scary when you're in work mode," Talullah said softly.

"I hate bringing you into this situation, but Cannon had a valid point that I can't shake." Scout adjusted his earpiece. This would be the last time he could speak to his team before going into Crystal's house.

They would be able to hear, but he wouldn't be able to hear them.

"Do you really believe Crystal could be helping Kyle?"

"If she believes it will get her closer to me, yes." Scout checked the weapon and handed it to Talullah. "I don't want to believe she'd fall for it, but some of the things she's done are a bit on the nutty side." He took in a long breath, letting it out slowly. "Are you sure you can handle this?"

"I've lived in Texas my entire life and how many times do I have to tell you that I have a permit and own my own gun? I know how to shoot. I'm good at it too."

"But aiming this thing at a person is different than an inanimate object."

Her eyes grew wide.

He pressed his earpiece. "Change in plans. Cannon, I'm sending Talullah to be with you."

"Negative," Cannon's voice echoed in his mind. "They will know something is up if she's not with you. Crystal either hinted she had to be there, or Kyle wants her there. We just don't know."

"I never agreed. Besides, don't you think it was weird that she even said her mom wanted to meet Talullah? If Kyle was listening, I would think he'd know that was bullshit."

"He might not know anything about her mother," Liam said.

Scout had to accept that was true. Crystal didn't talk about her too often. It was a painful topic in part because Crystal wasn't close to her mom for a lot of reasons. "That's true."

"And let's remember how well Crystal knows

you," Lance, another one of his teammates, said. "You wouldn't leave your girl behind in a situation like this. If Crystal is on our side, or with Kyle, you'll know pretty quickly, and then it will be three against one on the inside; you've got all of us out here. If not, we go to plan B."

"You know he's right," Liam said. Liam was always the fucking voice of reason.

"Fine. Let's get this party started," Scout mumbled.

"Don't forget the salsa," Lance said.

Talullah took the handgun and tucked it in her purse. "I'll be okay," she said. "In a matter of twenty minutes, you got this house surrounded."

"But I don't know what's going on inside. For all we know it could be booby-trapped."

"We've got your back," Liam said.

"I'm in the big tree across the street." Knox's voice came in loud and clear. "I've seen movement in the family room. That's about it. Everything else seems dark."

"I'm set up in the backyard," Huck said.

"This mission is a go." Cannon was down the street on the lookout for anyone or anything that might get in the way. Including the police. "On your mark, Scout."

"Removing my earpiece and heading to the front door." He slipped from behind the steering wheel and reached in the back for a bag of chips and salsa. Dumbest thing ever to actually bring the snack, but Cannon thought it might make the entrance through the front door go smoothly.

Scout met Talullah at the hood of his Jeep and took her hand. He squeezed. "Follow my lead and let me do all the talking."

"Kyle's going to want to hear from me."

"I don't give a shit what he wants and I know you don't want anyone telling you what to do, but this is my area expertise and I'm—"

"Scout. I'm going to listen and do what you say. I'm not too stupid to live."

"I would never call you stupid," he said. "Stubborn. Strong-willed. And maybe a dozen other descriptors. But not stupid."

"It's nice to know I'm falling head over heels for a smart man."

"You always manage to make me laugh." He pressed the doorbell and waited for what seemed like an eternity before Crystal inched open the door, barely showing her face.

Her eyes were bloodshot and her cheek bruised and swollen.

Scout let out an audible growl. He might not have any deep feelings left for Crystal, but that didn't mean he wanted to see her hurt.

She mouthed. *Sorry.* Then pulled back the door. She wore a vest lined with what looked like a bomb.

Kyle stood behind her with a small device in his hand.

Probably the trigger.

"You fucking bastard," Scout mumbled.

"I've got another vest like that for Talullah."

Scout swallowed. "You'll have to kill me before I let you strap a bomb on her."

"Oh, but Crystal is okay?"

"No. And trust me, you're going to pay for what you've done to her." Scout scanned the family room. Crystal had expensive taste, and that hadn't changed. Her furniture was custom and the wall art unique. She'd always been a neat freak, which he liked, and nothing in the room was out of place.

Maybe he could use that to his advantage.

"I think you're not grasping the fact that I'm the one in control." Kyle waved the device in his hand. "There is enough C4 on that vest to blow us all to bits."

"Then you'll be dead. What purpose does that serve?" Scout asked.

Talullah glanced at him with fear in her eyes.

Perhaps he shouldn't have reminded everyone of what that bomb could do. Time to move the conversation forward.

"Why are we here?" Scout asked. He needed to get his team as much information as quickly as possible. Although, the bomb situation added an element they hadn't thought about. Everything they'd come up with had been a basic hostage situation.

They'd dealt with those a million times.

Get in. Assess the situation. What's the fire power? Exit strategy? Possible causalities. Form a quick plan, take out the bad guy, and save the hostage.

Simple.

Not when you add C4 to the equation.

"Because you're my ticket out," Kyle said.

Scout handed the bag of chips and salsa to Talullah and inched closer to Crystal. He examined the vest without touching it. The wiring was simple. Barbaric actually. And unstable. Not that he was an expert, but he knew enough to know that this thing would go off like the Fourth of July the second Kyle engaged the trigger. "It's going to be okay," he whispered.

"Step back," Kyle ordered. "Both of you ladies take a seat on the sofa."

"Go ahead." Scout rubbed Talullah's biceps for a moment.

"Do you really think you're going to save the day?" Kyle asked. "Who the fuck do you think you are?"

Scout glanced between Crystal and Kyle. She'd always been more interested in the fact he was rich. Or came from a wealthy family. Not that he was Delta Force. That she could have lived without.

So, perhaps she hadn't told Kyle what he did.

"Just because you're in some special forces group, doesn't make you the brightest bulb in the closet," Kyle said. "I mean, you brought salsa."

Scout wanted to burst out laughing, but refrained. "What do you want?"

"The keys to your Jeep. Your wallet. And your gun."

There was no way Kyle was seriously going to make it this easy. He would be doing something crazy, like blowing them up the second he walked out the door.

"But before we do that, I need to make sure this little love triangle gets its justice." Kyle set the trigger on the table behind the couch and moved across the room.

"What the fuck does that mean?" Scout asked. This was his chance to make his move. He took the bag of salsa and chips from Talullah's grip and stood tall.

"It's pretty simple."

"Why don't you break it down for me."

"I guess you're all muscle, no brains," Kyle said.

"Something like that."

Kyle stood by the sofa with his hands on his hips. Talullah slipped her hand into her purse.

Scout eyed the device on the table and then shifted his gaze to Crystal, in hopes Talullah would know what that meant.

"All you need to know is that the two girls are going to kill each other, and you and I are going for a car ride."

Scout couldn't believe Kyle thought that would even fly, but he didn't have time to ponder what made Kyle tick. "You know, before we head out, I'm hungry and this is Crystal's favorite salsa." He lifted the bag to his right and swung, lunging forward.

The jar made contact with the side of Kyle's face. The glass shattered. A piece broke through the plastic bag, smashing into Kyle's skin. Blood trickled down his cheek.

"Motherfucker," Kyle yelled as he fell to the floor, landing flat on his back. He grabbed the side of his face. Blood seeped through his fingers as he shifted to a sitting position.

Talullah ran across the room with the vest in her hands. She quickly tugged it over his head.

"What the—?"

Scout pulled his weapon from his ankle holster. "Don't move, asshole." He took a quick glance over his shoulder. "Give me that, sweetheart."

Talullah handed him the trigger.

"Cannon, bring in the cavalry." Scout pressed the gun into the center of his chest. "I told you not to fucking move."

Three seconds later the front door blew open and Marco and Eddy came flying into the room, guns at the ready.

"Looks like you've got this under control," Marco said. "Just like your guy down the street said."

"You were listening with Cannon the entire time, weren't you?" Scout took a step back and let out a long breath. His heart continued to hammer in his chest.

"We were." Marco took out his handcuffs. "We'll take it from here."

"Are you okay?" Scout stood in front of Talullah and lifted her chin with his thumb and forefinger.

"I was scared out of my freaking mind, but yeah, I'm fine." She nodded. "I'm not sure Crystal is though." She jerked her head toward the sofa.

Crystal had collapsed into the cushions and covered her face. Her shoulders bobbed up and down.

"Hey," Scout said, kneeling in front of Crystal. "It's all over. You're safe now."

"You don't understand," Crystal said through her sobs. "I'm so sorry."

"It's okay. You don't have to apologize for anything."

She dropped her hands and stared at him. "But I've been spying on Talullah ever since she moved into that house."

"Excuse me? Why would he have you do that?" Talullah asked.

"He told me that he'd been seeing you for months, but that recently you started pulling away. He wondered if there had been another guy or something, and he wanted me to give him a few updates when I was visiting with Judy. So, when I saw Scout there, well—"

"You thought I was the other man," Scout said. "I have to know, was it Kyle's idea or yours to approach Talullah when I was deployed? And please be honest."

"Mine," Crystal said. "You can't blame a girl for trying."

"I'm sorry for what you went through here. No one should have to deal with all this." Scout helped Crystal to her feet. "But you have to understand you and I are over. For good. I care about Talullah, and she and I are together now."

"I get that." Crystal swiped at her cheeks. "I'm really sorry for my part in all this."

In the background, Kyle muttered a few obscenities as Eddy and Marco led him out of the house.

"Just take care of yourself." Scout leaned in and kissed her cheek. "The cops are going to need to take your statement."

"Hey. Thanks for bringing the salsa." Crystal smiled. "They're not so bad after all."

Talullah set some paper plates and napkins on the table in the back patio.

Scout reached out and grabbed her by the waist, pulling her to his lap. "Thanks for letting the team come over for pizza and wings."

"They saved a few lives today. It's the least I can do."

"You could have said no or told me to have it at my place and gone home alone."

She palmed his cheek. "There's no place I'd rather be than with you and if that means sometimes I have to share you with your team, then so be it."

He pressed his sweet lips on her shoulder. "They won't stay long. It's late. Everyone except Liam and Lance have wives or a family to get home to."

"Did you see the way Lance looked at Crystal?" Talullah asked.

"What are you talking about?"

"I saw it too." Cannon reached across the table and snagged a plate and then a couple slices of pizza. "And I think she gave him the once-over as well."

"That wouldn't be a good match." Scout laughed. "The man grew up in foster care and he lives in a trailer park."

"When it's true love, it changes everything." Talullah smiled.

"She's got a point." Cannon gave Scout a punch in the arm. "We'll have to have the two of you over for dinner. Maybe next weekend."

"Sounds good to me," Talullah said.

"How about the following weekend?" Scout rested his hand on her thigh. "My sister asked if I could come home this weekend and I wanted to know if you would join me."

"To meet your entire family?" Talullah cocked her head.

"That's my cue to leave." Cannon took his pizza and practically ran across the patio to where the rest of the team had sprawled out on the lawn.

"Yes," Scout said. "I wasn't sure if I was going to ask you or not, but after what happened an hour ago, I realized life is too short and since I want you in mine for a very long time, there's no time like the present to introduce you to my family."

"Does this mean I get another ride in the helicopter?"

He laughed. "It sure does."

"Okay. I'll go on one condition."

"What's that?"

"You have dinner with me and my family on Wednesday night."

"Oh. I might be working late that night," he said.

"Nope. He's not. I'll make sure of it." Cannon waved his hand over his head.

"Anyone ever tell you it's rude to listen in on other people's conversations?" Scout let out a long breath. "I guess you've got yourself a date. And possibly for many years to come."

"I look forward to exploring this relationship."

"Yeah, well, I look forward to when these clowns leave and I can explore you."

Talullah rested her head on his shoulder. Her future with Scout wasn't by any means set, but she could see one and it made her heart swell with the kind of love she never thought she'd ever experience.

Scout was her winding road and she was going to enjoy the ride.

EPILOGUE

FOUR MONTHS LATER...

Scout paced the ER waiting room. He couldn't think of anything worse than getting a text from his girlfriend asking him to meet her there as soon as possible.

"Hey, man," Wayne said as he stepped through the electric doors. "Come on back."

"What the hell is going on? Where's Talullah?"

Wayne raised his hands. "Boy, someone has their panties in a wad."

"So, she's okay?"

"She's fine." Wayne narrowed his gaze. "Why would you ask that?"

Scout lifted his hands toward the ceiling before letting them drop to his sides. "I don't know. Perhaps it's the random text she sent me in the middle of my day off asking me to come here as soon as I can, and then she doesn't respond to my texts or answer my calls."

"Sounds like you two had a breakdown in communication."

"No. It sounds like whatever my girlfriend is up to, you're in on it."

"I plead the fifth." Wayne led him to the doctors' lounge on the far end of the department. "She's in there."

Scout pulled open the door and found Talullah propped up on the couch with a pillow behind her back, sipping a ginger ale and munching on some crackers.

"What's going on?" He sat on the edge of the sofa, placing his hand on her knee. "Are you sick?"

"I had another dizzy spell."

"That's the third one this week."

She nodded. "This time I threw up." She waggled the can. "Which is why I'm drinking this and Wayne didn't think I should drive myself home at first."

"I agree with him."

"Well, that was until I took a test, and then we all realized I was fine, but I had already asked you to come, so here you are." She lifted a cracker and plopped it into his mouth.

He hadn't wanted one, but she didn't give him much of a choice. He chewed it, then took a sip of her drink.

"What test?"

"The one over there." She pointed. "Oh. And did you know that house over on Lampass River just went on the market?"

"I hadn't seen that." He cocked his head. "Since when did you start looking at properties for sale?"

"Since I took that test and Wayne made me put my feet up."

"You're freaking me out," Scout said. "What is wrong with you? What does this test tell you that you have?"

"It's not just me. I mean, I'm having it, but it's happening to us, and that got me thinking that maybe it's time to invoke the bigger, better house card with your parents."

"Have you been drinking in the middle of the day?" He pressed the back of his hand over her forehead.

"Nope. And there will be no more wine for me for a while."

"I'm so confused." Needing answers, he stood and strolled over to the counter in search of the paper-work for this test she took.

All he found was some stick thing with a positive sign on it. He took it in his hands and had a flashback to four months ago when he'd taken Talullah to meet his family for the first time and Hannah had also announced she was pregnant again.

Hannah had given their parents a similar gadget.

"Is this what I think it is?"

"If you're thinking it's a pregnancy test, then yes. That's exactly what it is." She crinkled her nose. "I know we've talked a lot about getting married lately. Even decided that maybe this summer would be a good time to do it. But we barely broached the kid conversation."

"No. We've had it. Decided two was good. Just never said when we'd do it." He held the stick up toward the light. Not that he wanted it to change, he just wanted to make sure it wouldn't.

His heart puffed out like a proud father.

A dad.

He was going to be a daddy.

Holy shit.

Tears burned his eyes. He set the test back on the counter and turned. "Is that house really for sale?"

"It is. But they want so much money for it."

"You do know we can afford it, right?"

"Not the point," she said. "But the master does have a purse closet."

"Oh. Well, we can't buy it then, because you really have a problem with purse spending. I'm going to have to cut you off."

"Better hope our little one isn't a girl."

"Lord help us," he said with a laugh as he sat on the edge of the sofa. "This isn't how I wanted to do this. I had an entire speech planned and the ring is back at the house—"

"Ring? You have an engagement ring?"

"I was planning on proposing tonight at dinner."

"Are you serious?"

"I wouldn't joke in an emergency room." He took her hand and kissed the back of it. "I love you, Talullah. I think I have since the moment we met. Will you do me the honor of marrying me?"

"Only if you put in our vows that you will love, honor, and buy me designer purses."

He dropped his head. "Yes, dear."

"I love you, Scout." She laughed. "You make my world a better place."

Thank you for taking the time to read *Shielding Talullah*. Please feel free to leave an honest review. *Sign up for my Newsletter (https://dl.bookfunnel.com/*

82gm 8b 9k 4y) where I often give away free books before publication.

Join my private Facebook group (https://www.facebook.com/groups/191706547909047/) where I post exclusive excerpts and discuss all things murder and love!

ALSO BY JEN TALTY

PROTECTING PRINCESS

PROTECTING MARLOWE

Love in the Adirondacks

AN INCONVENIENT FLAME

SHATTERED DREAMS

THE WEDDING DRIVER

Safe Harbor

MINE TO KEEP

MINE TO SAVE

Colorado Brotherhood Protectors

DEFENDING SPARROW

Legacy Series

DARK LEGACY

LEGACY OF LIES

SECRET LEGACY

With Me In Seattle

INVESTIGATE WITH ME

SAIL WITH ME

FLY WITH ME

THE LIGHTHOUSE

HER LAST HOPE

THE LAST FLIGHT

THE RETURN HOME

THE MATRIARCH

MAX & MILIAN

A CHRISTMAS MIRACLE

HOLIDAY'S VACATION

SPINNING WHEELS

The Collective Order

THE LOST SISTER

THE LOST SOLDIER

THE LOST SOUL

THE LOST CONNECTION

A Spin-Off Series: Witches Academy Series

THE NEW ORDER

The Brotherhood Protectors-Out of the Wild

ROUGH JUSTICE

ROUGH AROUND THE EDGES

ROUGH RIDE

ROUGH EDGE

ROUGH BEAUTY

The Brotherhood Protectors-The Saving Series

SAVING LOVE

SAVING MAGNOLIA

SAVING LEATHER

The Brotherhood Protectors

FAY'S SIX

Hot Hunks

Cove's Blind Date Blows Up

My Everyday Hero – Ledger

TEMPTING TAVOR

NEEDING NEOR

Holiday Romances

A CHRISTMAS GETAWAY

ALASKAN CHRISTMAS

WHISPERS

CHRISTMAS IN THE SAND

CHRISTMAS IN JULY

Heroes & Heroines on the Field

TAKING A RISK

TEE TIME

A New Dawn

THE BLIND DATE

SPRING FLING

SUMMER'S GONE

WINTER WEDDING

THE AWAKENING

The River Winery

RIVER'S EDGE

THE BURIED SECRET

IT'S IN HIS KISS

LIPS OF AN ANGEL

ABOUT THE AUTHOR

Jen Talty is the *USA Today* Bestselling Author of Contemporary Romance, Romantic Suspense, and Paranormal Romance. In the fall of 2020, her short story was selected and featured in a 1001 Dark Nights Anthology. She is currently contracted to write a new series with Kristen Proby's Lady Boss Press, as well as Susan Stoker's *Special Forces: Operation Alpha* and Elle James's *Brotherhood Protectors*.

Regardless of the genre, her goal is to take you on a ride that will leave you floating under the sun with warmth in your heart. She writes stories about broken heroes and heroines who aren't necessarily looking for romance, but in the end, they find the kind of love books are written about :).

She first started writing while carting her kids to one hockey rink after the other, averaging 170 games per year between 3 kids in 2 countries and 5 states. Her first book, IN TWO WEEKS was originally published in 2007. In 2010 she helped form a publishing company (Cool Gus Publishing) with *NY Times* Bestselling Author Bob Mayer where she ran the technical side of the business through 2016.

Jen is currently enjoying the next phase of her life… the empty nester! She and her husband reside in Jupiter, Florida.

Grab a glass of vino, kick back, relax, and let the romance roll in…

Sign up for my Newsletter (https://dl.bookfunnel.com/82gm8b9k4y) where I often give away free books before publication.

Join my private Facebook group (https://www.facebook.com/groups/191706547909047/) where I post exclusive excerpts and discuss all things murder and love!

Never miss a new release. Follow me on Amazon:amazon.com/author/jentalty
And on Bookbub: bookbub.com/authors/jen-talty

There are many more books in this fan fiction world than listed here, for an up-to-date list go to www.AcesPress.com

You can also visit our Amazon page at:
http://www.amazon.com/author/operationalpha

Special Forces: Operation Alpha World
Christie Adams: Charity's Heart
Linzi Baxter: Unlocking Dreams
Misha Blake: Flash
Anna Blakely: Rescuing Gracelynn
Julia Bright: Saving Lorelei
Cara Carnes: Protecting Mari
Kendra Mei Chailyn: Beast
Melissa Kay Clarke: Rescuing Annabeth
Samantha A. Cole: Handling Haven
Lorelei Confer: Protecting Sara
KaLyn Cooper: Spring Unveiled
Janie Crouch: Storm
Jordan Dane: Redemption for Avery
Tarina Deaton: Found in the Lost
Riley Edwards: Protecting Olivia
Dorothy Ewels: Knight's Queen
Lila Ferrari: Protecting Joy
Nicole Flockton: Protecting Maria

Hope Ford: Rescuing Karina

Michele Gwynn: Rescuing Emma

Desiree Holt: Protecting Maddie

Kris Jacen, Be With Me

Jesse Jacobson: Protecting Honor

Rayne Lewis: Justice for Mary

Callie Love & Ann Omasta: Hawaii Hottie

JM Madden: Rescuing Olivia

A.M. Mahler: Griffin

Ellie Masters: Sybil's Protector

Trish McCallan: Hero Under Fire

Rachel McNeely: The SEAL's Surprise Baby

KD Michaels: Saving Laura

Olivia Michaels: Protecting Harper

Annie Miller: Securing Willow

Keira Montclair: Wolf and the Wild Scots

MJ Nightingale: Protecting Beauty

Melinda Owens: Betraying Katie

Victoria Paige: Reclaiming Izabel

Danielle Pays: Defending Sarina

Lainey Reese: Protecting New York

KeKe Renée: Protecting Bria

TL Reeve and Michele Ryan: Extracting Mateo

Deanna L. Rowley: Saving Veronica

Angela Rush: Charlotte

Rose Smith: Saving Satin

Lynne St. James: SEAL's Spitfire
Sarah Stone: Shielding Grace
Jen Talty: Burning Desire
Reina Torres, Rescuing Hi'ilani
LJ Vickery: Circus Comes to Town
R. C. Wynne: Shadows Renewed

Delta Team Three Series
Lori Ryan: Nori's Delta
Becca Jameson: Destiny's Delta
Lynne St James, Gwen's Delta
Elle James: Ivy's Delta
Riley Edwards: Hope's Delta

Police and Fire: Operation Alpha World
Freya Barker: Burning for Autumn
B.P. Beth: Scott
Jane Blythe: Salvaging Marigold
Julia Bright, Justice for Amber
Hadley Finn: Exton
Emily Gray: Shelter for Allegra
Alexa Gregory: Backdraft
Deanndra Hall: Shelter for Sharla
Jenna Harte: Dead But Not Forgotten
India Kells: Shadow Killer
Amber Kuhlman: Protecting Paisley

Reina Torres: Justice for Sloane
Aubree Valentine, Justice for Danielle
Maddie Wade: Finding English
Laine Vess: Justice for Lauren

Tarpley VFD Series

Silver James, Fighting for Elena
Deanndra Hall, Fighting for Carly
Haven Rose, Fighting for Calliope
MJ Nightingale, Fighting for Jemma
TL Reeve, Fighting for Brittney
Nicole Flockton, Fighting for Nadia

As you know, this book included at least one character from Susan Stoker's books. To check out more, see below.

SEAL Team Hawaii Series

Finding Elodie

Finding Lexie

Finding Kenna

Finding Monica

Finding Carly (Oct 2022)

Finding Ashlyn (Feb 2023)

Finding Jodelle (July 2023)

Eagle Point Search & Rescue

Searching for Lilly

Searching for Elsie

Searching for Bristol (Nov 2022)

Searching for Caryn (April 2023)

Searching for Finley (TBA)

Searching for Heather (TBA)

Searching for Khloe (TBA)

The Refuge Series

Deserving Alaska (Aug 2022)

Deserving Henley (Jan 2023)

Deserving Reese (May 2023)
Deserving Cora (TBA)
Deserving Lara (TBA)
Deserving Maisy (TBA)
Deserving Ryleigh (TBA)

Delta Team Two Series

Shielding Gillian
Shielding Kinley
Shielding Aspen
Shielding Jayme (novella)
Shielding Riley
Shielding Devyn
Shielding Ember
Shielding Sierra

SEAL of Protection: Legacy Series

Securing Caite (FREE!)
Securing Brenae (novella)
Securing Sidney
Securing Piper
Securing Zoey
Securing Avery
Securing Kalee
Securing Jane

Delta Force Heroes Series

Rescuing Rayne (FREE!)

Rescuing Aimee (novella)

Rescuing Emily

Rescuing Harley

Marrying Emily (novella)

Rescuing Kassie

Rescuing Bryn

Rescuing Casey

Rescuing Sadie (novella)

Rescuing Wendy

Rescuing Mary

Rescuing Macie (novella)

Rescuing Annie

Badge of Honor: Texas Heroes Series

Justice for Mackenzie (FREE!)

Justice for Mickie

Justice for Corrie

Justice for Laine (novella)

Shelter for Elizabeth

Justice for Boone

Shelter for Adeline

Shelter for Sophie

Justice for Erin

Justice for Milena

Shelter for Blythe

Justice for Hope

Shelter for Quinn

Shelter for Koren

Shelter for Penelope

SEAL of Protection Series

Protecting Caroline (FREE!)

Protecting Alabama

Protecting Fiona

Marrying Caroline (novella)

Protecting Summer

Protecting Cheyenne

Protecting Jessyka

Protecting Julie (novella)

Protecting Melody

Protecting the Future

Protecting Kiera (novella)

Protecting Alabama's Kids (novella)

Protecting Dakota

New York Times, USA Today and *Wall Street Journal* Bestselling Author Susan Stoker has a heart as big as the state of Tennessee where she lives, but this all American girl has also spent the last fourteen years living in Missouri, California, Colorado, Indiana, and Texas. She's married to a retired Army man who now gets to follow *her* around the country.

www.stokeraces.com
www.AcesPress.com
susan@stokeraces.com

Made in United States
Cleveland, OH
04 December 2025

27509147R00154